D0975665

TAKING UP SPACE

Gerber, Alyson, author.
Taking up space

2021
33305251895342
cu   05/19/21

TAKING UP SPACE

ALYSON GERBER

SCHOLASTIC PRESS
NEW YORK CITY

Copyright © 2021 by Alyson Gerber

All rights reserved. Published by Scholastic Press, an imprint of Scholastic Inc.,
Publishers since 1920. SCHOLASTIC, SCHOLASTIC PRESS, and associated logos
are trademarks and/or registered trademarks of Scholastic Inc.

The publisher does not have any control over and does not assume any responsibility
for author or third-party websites or their content.

No part of this publication may be reproduced, stored in a retrieval system, or
transmitted in any form or by any means, electronic, mechanical, photocopying,
recording, or otherwise, without written permission of the publisher. For information
regarding permission, write to Scholastic Inc., Attention: Permissions Department,
557 Broadway, New York, NY 10012.

This book is a work of fiction. Names, characters, places, and incidents are either the
product of the author's imagination or are used fictitiously, and any resemblance to
actual persons, living or dead, business establishments, events,
or locales is entirely coincidental.

Library of Congress Cataloging-in-Publication Data available
ISBN 978-1-338-18600-0

1 2021

Printed in the U.S.A.   23
First edition, May 2021
Book design by Baily Crawford

To Juliette

ONE

I SPRINT TOWARD the basket and V-cut to get open, but the player guarding me, number twelve with the pigtail braids, is quick and no matter how hard I push myself, I can't break free.

Ryan dribbles up the court, weaving the ball between her legs. She crosses over left, then right, and dodges her defender before passing the ball to Ines, who's standing on the other side of the three-point line.

I need to get open. I try again—I cut in, sprint out, and manage to make enough space for Ines to hand the ball to me. I drive to the basket, shoot a layup, and score. *Boom. Two points! Yes!*

A few people in the stands cheer. There's a pretty big crowd today. It's normally just parents and siblings, but the girls' JV team and both boys' basketball teams stayed to watch our game, because we're playing our biggest rivals.

Benny is sitting in the front row wearing jeans, a gray hoodie, and his new thick-rimmed glasses that make him look cute and smart at the same time. He smiles at me, and I'm thankful that I'm already sweaty and red, so he can't see that I'm blushing.

Duke pushes his blond hair off his pale face and whispers something to Benny. They laugh. Duke is the kind of boy that everyone agrees is cute. His cuteness is a fact. He's like the chocolate chip cookie of boys. But I like the way Benny looks better. I turn away from them and take a deep breath. I need to focus. I can't get distracted by my crush when I'm trying to win.

I high-five Ryan and Ines and then sprint to the other end of the court. By the time I get there, I'm gasping for air. I never used to heave like this.

The game is tied. But there's still time for us to win, and I know we can. It doesn't matter that the other girls are taller and more athletic. We're a stronger team.

I stay on number twelve as she cuts in and out, and ignore

my achy chest and the cramp on my right side that's probably from not drinking enough water. We all need to play tight defense if we're going to beat this team, and I want to more than anything.

"Ry, screen right," I shout.

She maneuvers fast and dodges the pick.

There's something that happens to me when I'm on the court, when I'm cutting and guarding and working to win—I know for sure I matter, and that I'm important to our team. It's not hard for me to say what I need in basketball, because the rules are clear. Everyone has to speak up to support one another so we can play our best. I never want the game to end.

I don't stand too close to number twelve. I've already fouled three times since Coach Lemon put me in at the start. If I foul two more times, I'm out for the game.

Fouling isn't always a bad thing. It can be. But it happens when you guard close and play aggressively, which I do. Only something feels off again today. It's been like this since basketball season started five weeks ago, like my hands and feet aren't mine. Every time I try to block a shot I end up accidentally bumping into the shooter or stepping into where they're jumping, making it hard for them to land. Number twelve shouldn't be able to outrun me, but it feels like I can't keep up. I need to get my head in the game.

I'm one of the strongest players on the team. My best friend, Ryan, and I both play hard and crush it on the court. Basketball is my number one favorite thing ever. It's Ryan's too. We've been practicing a lot, after school and on weekends with her older twin brothers, Max and Everett, who are getting college basketball scholarships. They're juniors now, and they already have a bunch of really good offers. All they have to do is commit to a school. Ryan and I both want to play in college one day too.

I shuffle across the court, watching number twelve and listening to my teammates.

When I step back, I drill into someone. My sneakers squeak against the floor, and I barely catch myself from falling over.

I didn't know she was there. No one called out the screen.

The ref blows the whistle and calls a foul on me—another one. One more and I'm out. I look over at Coach Lemon, because I know there's a chance she'll replace me. But she doesn't wave me over. *Everything is fine.*

There are only two minutes left in the game. And we have to win. The more we win, the longer the season lasts and the more games we get to play, and I need as much basketball as I can get.

The girl I ran over inbounds the ball.

I play tight defense without fouling and make it impossible for number twelve to get near the hoop. My teammates are working as hard as they can too. We get a stop, but when we get the ball back, the other team starts face-guarding us.

It's hard to make space. When Emilia tries to pass to me, number twelve intercepts it and starts up the court with her right hand, and then, *whoop*, switches to her left hand, runs around Emilia, and before I can recover, she goes cross-court to one of her teammates.

Ryan lunges forward seemingly out of nowhere and steals the ball back. She sprints toward their hoop, and before anyone else can catch up to her, she lays it in and scores!

Err. Err. The buzzer goes off.

We won!

"Yes!" I shout.

Ryan runs over and hugs me as hard as she can, then we high-five, low-five, pivot-turn, and fist-bump. It's our BFF-totally-not-bragging-too-much-just-celebrating victory handshake. I can't stop smiling.

"We're so getting into the Hall of Fame!" She grins.

"You know it," I say. And even though I feel a little weird about how I played, our team won, and that has to matter more than anything else.

After the game, Mom drives Ryan, Emilia, and me to our house for a sleepover. We usually go to Ryan's on Fridays, which is the best thing ever, because the Martins have an entire refrigerator in the basement filled with snacks, and in the morning her dad makes fluffy-in-the-middle chocolate chip pancakes from scratch and scrambled eggs with multiple cheeses. Just one time, I wish Mom or Dad would make a big breakfast and that our house would smell like bacon and buttery French toast. But that's never going to happen.

We couldn't go to Ryan's tonight because her parents took her brothers to visit a college in Connecticut. And Emilia isn't allowed to have friends at her house. So, mine is the only option if we want to hang out, which we obviously do.

I'm still not sure why Emilia's parents won't let her have friends over. Her house is way bigger than Ryan's and mine put together. They probably wouldn't even notice us. I just feel sort of weird asking her to explain. Emilia doesn't talk about her family. Not that we sit around talking about our families or anything, because we definitely don't do that. *Boring.* But it seems different with her, like they're off-limits. I'm not exactly sure, because we're new best friends. Emilia moved to our town outside Boston from Minneapolis at the beginning of the year. On the first day of seventh grade, she sat down next to Ryan and me in homeroom and started talking about the WNBA playoffs, and we clicked, like we were all totally meant to be besties.

Most of the time, it's like Emilia has always been in our group, but right now, it seems like I'm missing important pieces of information about her, which makes me feel like I don't actually know her at all. I guess new best friends are different than best friends you've known your whole life.

Usually, I hate having sleepovers at my house, because the whole time I'm worried my friends will notice how weird Mom is about food or they'll ask for snacks when there aren't any. But I'm excited for tonight, because I already know we won't have that problem. This morning, I gave Mom a shopping list. **Sarah's Sleepover Snacks: 1. Doritos 2. Cheez-Its 3. Oreos 4. Popcorn 5. Potato chips 6. Honey Nut Cheerios 7. Chex 8. Frosted Flakes.**

Mom goes to the grocery store every day. And now she knows exactly what to buy. So, no weird food stuff today.

Once we're at my house, we drop our bags in the den and then go into the kitchen to grab water. We all need to hydrate before we head outside to shoot hoops. My stomach cramps up when I see the groceries on the counter—one bag of Doritos, a box of Chex, almonds, apples, milk, and eggs.

Most of the stuff on my list is missing, and there's no chance Mom already put some food away. The only thing that's ever in our cabinets is coffee, spices, a box of pasta that expired in September, and candy.

I mean, I'm lucky. We have money for food. Not everyone does. I know there are so many kids whose parents would remember to follow their lists but can't always afford to, and that's unfair and hard in a much bigger way than what happens to me. I think maybe I feel extra bad, because I know what it feels like to be hungry at home.

I don't say anything to Mom when she walks back into the kitchen, because I don't want Ryan and Emilia to notice I'm upset. But it doesn't make sense. This time, I wrote down exactly what I wanted. She didn't need to guess or think or remember. I used to just ask Mom for generic categories of food, like chips and cereal. I thought that would be easier than asking her to look for specific brands. But she barely ever bought what I wanted then either. And when I told her I needed snacks for after practice, because it was hard to wait for dinner, she started serving dinner earlier, which was great, until there was nothing to eat when I got hungry before bed. I've tried everything. But there's never enough food.

I open the fridge and take out three water bottles. There isn't much of anything on the translucent shelves, just a few plain, nonfat yogurts, salad dressing, a shriveled lemon, and what's left of last night's dinner—salmon and vegetables.

Mom always buys exactly what she thinks we need for breakfast and dinner. If she were cooking tonight, there would be fish or chicken and some kind of vegetable. But we're ordering pizza for the sleepover, so there's even less food.

When Dad is here, things are different—less empty. But he's not here.

I close the fridge before my friends have a chance to see.

"What are you girls doing to celebrate your big win?" Mom asks.

"Shooting around," Ryan says.

Mom smiles and then picks up the milk like she's about to put the carton away.

"I'll meet you outside," I say to my friends, because I want them to leave before Mom opens the fridge.

"Cool," Emilia says.

"Is it okay if we take these?" Ryan points to the Doritos on the counter.

"Totally," I say, like it's no big deal, and that's definitely not our only bag.

"Thanks," she says, taking the chips with her.

I wait until I hear the door close before I turn to Mom and say, "I made you a list."

"The store didn't have everything, sweetheart." She opens the fridge and puts the milk and eggs away. "I got what they had."

"But you could have bought other snacks, instead of no snacks. It's just not enough food for a sleepover." My words come out too loud.

"I'm sorry." Her eyebrows knit together, like she really doesn't know how to fix the problem.

It feels good to hear she's sorry. But it doesn't actually make this better for me. Snacks aren't going to magically appear.

"I got us two new books at the library." Mom changes the subject.

"Agatha Christie?" I ask.

She nods. "I found out about another mystery author I think we're really going to like. She's British too. Only new and modern. Sharna Jackson. There's a short waiting list for her books at the library. I added our names."

I smile. "I can't wait!"

Mom and I both love detective novels. They're sort of our thing. Well, mysteries were my thing and then Mom got into them too—for me. When I was little, we used to read them out loud before bed. We started with Clubhouse Mysteries, the Boxcar Children, Encyclopedia Brown, and eventually worked our way up to Nancy Drew and Agatha Christie. Somewhere along the way, stories with puzzles and clues and problems to solve became both our favorites. We read two books at the same time and switch off, trading back and forth.

"Peter at the library recommended *The Clocks* and *The Mirror Crack'd from Side to Side*. Which one do you want to start with?"

"Who are the detectives?"

"Poirot is in *The Clocks* and Marple is in *The Mirror*."

"*The Clocks*," I say.

Mom grins. "I already started reading *The Mirror*."

"How did you know?" I ask.

She rubs my shoulder. "You always pick Poirot."

I don't understand why Mom is so good at getting me books and so bad at getting me food.

I meet my friends outside. It's warm for January, and we

haven't had any snow yet this year, so Ryan and Emilia don't have to clear off the pavement before they draw lines with chalk.

Ryan opens the chips and starts eating. She's long and lean, like a beanpole, even under her puffy coat.

"You're up first." Emilia passes me the ball.

I stand at the top of the makeshift perimeter. I won the last round of H-O-R-S-E, which means I get to start. I usually win, unless Ryan's brothers decide they want to play too. I don't let myself think too hard. It's going in. I can feel it. I spin, dribble twice—*thump, thump*—shoot, follow through. *Swish.*

"Woo-hoo!" Ryan shouts. "There she is—the real deal Sarah Weber! We're going to take home the championship and make the seventh-grade Hall of Fame."

I force myself to smile. The Hall of Fame is a glass cabinet outside the gym with pictures of all the teams that have won championships. Our picture from last year is there. Ryan's brothers won three seasons in a row, and she's determined to do the same. I am too. Only after the game, I'm sort of scared that can't happen.

"Something's wrong." Emilia looks at me, like she's worried I'm not okay.

"No." I shake my head. "I don't know. I didn't play my best today. Everything felt off."

"Fact. You're amazing at hoops," Emilia says. "It's just that you're pretty competitive, which you should be. But that's probably why you're being hard on yourself."

I shrug. "Maybe."

"Trust me. I'm definitely right." I don't mind that Emilia can be a little in your face. I never have to worry about her talking behind my back, since she says everything she's thinking out loud. It almost makes me want to say everything I'm thinking too.

"Everyone has cold streaks, even WNBA players," Ryan says. "You just have to get your confidence back. And I mean, you didn't play your best, and you still scored six points, which rocks."

I nod and try to trust her, because Ryan sounds sure of herself and like she definitely has all the answers about basketball.

"Your shooting is so legit," Emilia says.

I smile, because I know that's true, and it feels like a reason to believe that nothing has changed and I'm still the same. I can shoot, and I'm fast. I just had a weird start to the season. But it doesn't mean anything.

"You're up." I pass the ball to Ryan.

She catches it, then takes more chips. "Sustenance. Then basketball."

"Good call." I grab a handful of chips too, finish them off, and go back for more. Spicy Nacho Doritos are my number one favorite snack. But I stop myself. I'm afraid if I take too many we'll finish them before the pizza gets here, and Ryan or Emilia will ask me to grab another bag, which doesn't exist.

I'm not sure what time Mom placed the delivery order. Part of me is scared she forgot since Dad is away on a business trip until tomorrow, and sometimes when he's traveling or out to dinner with a client, when it's just us, Mom forgets about dinner. I'm not enough for her to always remember the next meal. I really hope that Ryan and Emilia being here reminded her to call the restaurant and that the pizzas show up soon.

Ryan eats the chips in her hand, wipes the orange stuff off her fingers, and then takes her shot. The ball bounces off the glass, circles the rim, and falls over the edge. "No!" she yells.

Emilia runs after the ball. She rests it between her sneakers while she pulls her thick black waves into a perfect side pony. She unzips her jacket, tugs on her jersey and sports bra, and adjusts her pants. Once she's done rearranging her clothes, she looks comfortable again and ready to play, like her curves belong to her. Mine look like they're glued onto my body. Or maybe that's just how they feel. I want to ask her how long it takes to get used to having everything about you be different, because she's had her period forever and her body changed way before she moved here, which makes her an expert compared to me. But Emilia is one of those confident people. She's always proud and happy to be exactly who she is, so I don't think she'd understand the question, because she's probably never felt awkward or like she didn't fit inside herself ever. She steps up to the line, dribbles, shoots, and misses completely.

"Grr. I'm laying bricks today." She stomps her foot. "Whatever."

Ryan and Emilia both have H, tied for second place, because they missed a shot, and I'm in the lead with no letters. I know beating them at H-O-R-S-E doesn't mean anything, but I still want to win.

It's my turn again. I run up to the basket, and when I get under the hoop, I jump off my right foot and make a left-handed reverse layup. I act like it's easy for me, even though it isn't easy for any of us since we're all right-handed, but it's especially hard for Ryan. She isn't very strong on her left side ever since last summer when she broke her arm messing around on a trampoline.

"Ugh. You would!" Ryan says to me as the House of Pizza van pulls up and parks in front of the driveway.

"Lucky break," I say, and nod toward the van, when really I know I'm the lucky one, because Mom remembered dinner. I didn't have to sneak away from my friends to ask her to order, or explain to them why the food is late, or distract them from the fact that every meal at my house is hard.

We collect our things and follow the salty smell of melted cheese into the kitchen.

Mom puts plates and silverware in the middle of the table and the food on the counter. She smiles at me, but under her thin frames her blue eyes look tired, like she's had enough for the day.

Mom is tiny, and she has the kind of beautiful and unusual face that strangers comment on. My face is like Dad's. Nothing about me is striking. I'm regular and fine enough, but looking average doesn't bother me that much, because I'm great at basketball. I can always help my team. It makes up for the fact that at home Mom won't buy the food I ask for even when I write it down, and sometimes she forgets I need to eat if Dad isn't home, and I have no say in anything that happens to me. On the court, *I* get to decide how things go.

"Just leave your plates in the sink. I'll clean everything up later," Mom says. Then she opens *The Mirror*, leaning against the counter, like she can't wait another second to find out what's going to happen next, but also, it kind of feels like she's watching us and keeping track of what we're eating.

I don't realize until I start to take food that there are two salads but only one small pie, which isn't good.

"I need a lot of pizza tonight," Ryan says between bites. "My stomach is seriously eating itself."

"Mine too!" Emilia sprinkles red pepper flakes all over her food.

I try my slice. It's everything I want it to be—crunchy on the bottom, soft on top. The cheese is warm and the sauce isn't too sweet. I never want this meal to end.

"This is ridiculously good," Emilia says. "BTW, PMS is real and the only thing that helps is so much pizza."

"Truth," I say.

Emilia smiles at me.

Ryan takes another big bite. She doesn't want to talk about periods, because she doesn't have hers yet, which I think is lucky and she thinks is embarrassing. I don't get how we can see the same thing the exact opposite way, but it's been happening a lot lately, so I should probably get used to it.

"I think we need more pizza," Ryan whispers to me.

"Me too," I say softly, and then before I can stop myself, I ask, "Mom, could we maybe order another pizza?"

She glances up from her book. "There's still a lot left."

Ryan and Emilia look at each other in this way I've never seen or maybe I've just never noticed before, like they're in on something and I'm not.

"There are only two more slices," I say back. "And we're all really hungry—because of the game."

"Oh. Sure," Mom says. "If you think you need more, I can call right now."

"We do," I say.

"Would it be okay if we got pepperoni?" Emilia asks. "It's my number one fave."

"Mine too!" Ryan says.

"Of course." Mom acts like she doesn't care what kind of pizza we get. Only her voice is strained, so I know she doesn't approve of pepperoni. I really hope Ryan and Emilia can't tell.

"Can we please get a large this time?" I ask.

"Really?" Mom looks surprised. "You're *that* hungry?"

I swallow, and even though I feel deflated and it's hard for me to say anything right now, I force myself to answer, "Yes." I don't get how I can be so aggressive on the court but I can barely ask Mom for a second pizza that I know for sure we all need.

"We can definitely eat a large," Ryan backs me up.

Mom nods. "Okay."

"But fingers crossed there are leftover slices," Emilia adds. "I heart cold pizza in the a.m."

"Samesies!" Ryan says.

I take a deep breath, because now at least there might be something for breakfast.

I don't turn away from Mom until I see her pick up the phone and place the order.

When she hangs up, she says, "The pizza should be here in a half hour. I already paid the bill and the tip. I'll be in my room if you need anything."

"Thanks, Dr. Weber," Ryan says.

"You're welcome. You girls have fun." Mom turns around and walks away down the long hall toward her room.

The pizza gets here pretty fast, and it's a large! *Phew!*

I'm pretty sure that only happened because Ryan agreed with me about the size in front of Mom. But I try not to think about what I'd be eating if my friends weren't here.

We all dig in. It's a little easier to block out Mom's opinions about pepperoni when I'm with Ryan and Emilia, because they both love eating so much.

We each have two more slices, and for the first time since Dad left on Monday, I'm full at the end of a meal at home.

After we're done with dinner, we shower, change, and go into the family room, because it's bigger than my room and far away from Mom, which means she won't be able to hear us talking and laughing and staying up late.

"Let's play Heads Up!" Emilia says.

"I'm in," I say. I like any kind of game, as long as it's fun and there's a little competition. That's something Emilia and I have in common. Ryan doesn't want to compete unless she knows for sure she can win.

"Fine," Ryan says. "But I'm not playing the movie-star deck or whatever. It's boring, and I never know who any of those old actor peeps are."

"Deal," Emilia says to Ryan, and then looks at me. "You start." She opens the app and hands me her phone.

I hold the screen up to my forehead.

"One of the most important inventors like ever," Emilia says.

"Alexander Graham Bell?" I guess.

They shake their heads at the same time.

"Albert Einstein?" I try again.

"Nope," Emilia says. "This guy was a total hottie alert."

"Tesla!" I shout.

"Yes!" they shout back.

"Wait. Time-out. Tesla was hot?" Ryan asks.

"Duh!" Emilia says. "He's the Benny Saraf of famous inventors."

Ryan shakes her head and makes a face. "I know you like him, but I don't get why. I guess he's just not my type."

"He's everyone's type. I mean, he's so cute and, like, mature." Emilia is right, but I don't back her up. She doesn't know about my crush on Benny. Ryan used to know. I told her I liked him in fifth grade, but I'm pretty sure she forgot by now or maybe she thinks I'm over him, because ever since Emilia announced her crush, neither of us has mentioned mine. It feels weird to like-like the same person as Emilia. But I can't help who I like. If I could, I would definitely pick someone else. I don't want to be in competition with my bestie for a boy, even if he is really cute and smart and nice to everyone. "You never have a crush," Emilia says to Ryan.

"What's your point?" Ryan asks.

"I bet you like someone, and you're not telling us who." She crosses her arms over her chest. "Is it Benny? I pinkie-promise I won't be mad if it is. It's not like you can call dibs on a boy. That's not a thing. Boys aren't like chairs." I want to tell Emilia about my crush. She just said she wouldn't be mad at Ryan, so she wouldn't be mad at me either. But I don't say anything. It doesn't even matter that I like him, because there's a zero percent chance he likes me back.

Ryan rolls her eyes. "I don't have a crush on Benny. You're the only one who's obsessed with him."

"Mm-hmm. Doubt it," Emilia says to Ryan. Then she looks at me. "So, what else do you have for snacks?"

"Um, I'm not sure." I look down at the red-and-navy pattern on the rug and pull my knees into my chest, because almonds probably don't count. I wish that Mom had listened to me and bought a lot of snacks like I asked her to, or that we were at Ryan's house so we could raid the fridge in the basement. "I mean, I don't think we have anything else."

"Really?" Emilia tilts her head, looking confused.

"Hold up." Ryan opens the cabinet under the TV, reaches

behind a stack of books, and pulls out a giant bag of Kit Kats and an already-opened bag of Peppermint Patties that have been there for a while. Normally, I hate that there's candy hidden in every corner of our house—tucked away in Mom's vanity and stashed between fancy plates in our dining room drawers. But right now I'm so happy the candy is here, because my friends have something else to eat. And it feels like proof that everything is fine. There can't be a real problem, because look—we have so much junk food.

"Where did those come from?" Emilia asks.

Ryan looks at me, like I'm supposed to explain that if you search long and hard enough you can find almost any kind of candy you want in my house. Mom barely ever eats it. I guess she just likes knowing the candy is there, in case she ever wants some. But I don't know how to explain why we never have enough food but we always have plenty of candy.

I'm pretty sure Mom doesn't have an eating disorder, because she doesn't fit into the categories we learned about in health class. Also, I did some googling and she doesn't have a lot of the symptoms. I mean, she's definitely weird about food, but she eats almost everything, except beef, because she got sick from a hamburger when she was pregnant with me, and fried food, because she says it's not healthy, and a few other things, like pepperoni. She doesn't make herself sick or binge or exercise every day. I'm just pretty sure I wouldn't think so much about what I'm going to eat or when or how if Mom didn't make food hard to come by.

I don't say any of that out loud. Instead, I say, "My mom is really into candy," because even though Ryan and Emilia are my best friends, I don't feel like talking or thinking about Mom or food when I don't have to.

"That's awesome," Emilia says. "I wish my mom were like that. It's totally wasted on you. You hate candy." She stops herself like maybe she's putting the pieces together. "Wait, so, why don't you have any regular snacks?"

"It's like their family thing," Ryan says. "They basically never have any food, except candy."

It surprises me, because I didn't know Ryan thought that, but maybe she's right and it is just our family thing.

I nod, like it's no big deal, because I really don't want it to matter.

TWO

ON MONDAY AT SCHOOL, my pants feel tight. As soon as I'm inside the lobby, I stop walking and pretend to read the poster on the wall about Chef Junior—the YouTube cooking competition that's being filmed at our school in a few weeks—while I adjust my clothes. Only nothing I do actually helps. Every time I move, I can feel the fabric tugging, like parts of me have shifted again overnight. I wish I'd picked a different outfit with room to breathe so I could walk down the hall without feeling like I'm suffocating.

Ryan and Emilia and a few other girls from the basketball team are standing by the bathrooms huddled around Tamar.

Tamar is the kind of pretty and perfectly accessorized I wish I could be. Her nails are painted purple with a yellow design, like Easter eggs, that looks pretty against her olive skin, and the polish doesn't exactly go with her slouchy top, leggings, and suede sneakers, but the whole outfit looks like it belongs together in this casual way, like being cool is easy for her. "I'm so not in the mood for health."

"Seriously." Sage flips her blonde waves. "It's awkward."

"Totes," Emilia says. She's sort of friends with Tamar and Sage, not like super close or anything, but she's new, so she tries with everyone.

"All that openness really freaks me out," Sage says. "Some people take the opportunity to share their feelings a little too seriously. It's like, hello . . . TMI."

"Like who?" Emilia asks.

Sage, Tamar, and I are all in the same class. But I'm not sure who she's talking about. I know it's not me, because I barely talk in class.

"We're not supposed to name people," Sage says. "Remember? Honor code."

"Oh yeah." Emilia acts like she forgot. Only I don't think she did.

"So, anyway, random question, who's auditioning for Chef

Junior?" Sage looks around the circle, getting ready to size up the competition.

Ryan shakes her head. "I don't like to cook. I just like to eat."

"Same," I say quickly. Only it's not the same at all, because I don't know if I like to cook. I've never tried. One time, I asked Mom to teach me how to make scrambled eggs. They're one of the non-candy foods she likes. She said she would, but every time I reminded her, she pushed it off, and I got the hint that she wanted me to stop asking. But I don't need anyone finding out that I've never cooked. Ryan and Emilia already know my mom is weird about food, and I don't want them to think I am too.

"My parents won't sign the release form," Emilia says. "They don't want me on YouTube or something. It's dumb."

"Bummer," Tamar says, like she actually feels really bad for Emilia.

"You need to do something about that," Sage says. "Tell them it's going to be huge. Chef Emily Ying is coming here. She's so famous. I can't believe they're filming at our school. I mean, I know Duke's dad is a producer, but still. T and I are getting on the show and become cooking influencers.

Like the peeps on those posters around school, but, you know, actually cool."

"Sababa," Tamar says to Sage, and they high-five. It seems like she's talking in a secret code, but she's actually speaking Hebrew. Her dad is Israeli, and she knows a few words that she sprinkles into conversation.

The bell rings.

Everyone rushes to first period.

I follow Tamar and Sage down the hall, but the second Emilia and Ryan are gone, they forget I exist. They've always been like that to me. Not mean. Just not interested. I wish I could be the kind of person who didn't care or notice that they ignore me, but I'm not. I can't help how much it hurts. It feels like what they think of me matters more than ever, because Emilia is friends with them and I guess Ryan is sort of friends with them too, and I don't want to be the only one who isn't.

When I get to health, I can see Benny out of the corner of my eye, sitting in the back row. I basically always know when he's in a room. I'm careful never to look directly at him, like he's the sun or an eclipse or something that could hurt me. I need to protect myself. He can't know I like him. No one can, because of Emilia.

Benny seems older than other boys in our grade, even though his birthday is March 2, which is basically in the middle of the year. I'm pretty sure it's because he's mature, and also because he has armpit hair, which not every boy in our grade has yet. I mean, more of them might have that by now. It's hard to tell since it's cold outside and everyone is wearing long sleeves. Not that I'm specifically looking or keeping track, but sometimes you can see it during gym or when people raise their hands in class. Benny has had armpit hair since the beginning of sixth grade. He was one of the first to get it. Ryan and I both noticed right away. I used to think it was weird for people to have armpit hair, and now I think it's weird when they don't. I'm not really sure when that changed, but it feels like it happened out of nowhere, and like maybe it means something bigger about me and how everything about me keeps changing.

There are name tags at each seat, which are new and strange, since Coach Lemon is our teacher and she doesn't usually assign seats. She doesn't need to have a lot of rules, like other teachers, because everyone pays attention in her class. I get that I'm biased, since she's my favorite coach ever, but she's the best.

I walk around the room and look for my name, trying not to think about how the front button on my jeans is digging into me. I'm not sure when my pants stopped fitting right. But it's like all of a sudden, I can't count on anything to be the way it used to be anymore, not even me.

Ines is sitting in the second-to-last row, reviewing her sheet music. Auditions for the seventh-grade play are this week. And even though she's so good at playing center in basketball since she's the tallest girl in our grade and it's basically impossible to stop her from scoring, musical theater is her passion. She's always singing in the locker room, which I think is cool, even if some girls on the team think musicals are for dorks.

I can't find my name.

"Sarah." I don't need to look up to know it's Benny. I have his voice memorized. My cheeks flush, and my heart beats hard. It's so loud I'm afraid other people might actually be able to hear how much I like him. "Sarah."

I think about pretending I didn't hear him so he'll say my name a third time, because he makes *Sarah* sound special and pretty, and like maybe he thinks I'm those things too. Only I'm not sure where Tamar and Sage are sitting, and if they're close, I don't want them to hear Benny or notice I'm blushing and figure out how I feel about him. So, I take a breath and look up.

His eyes are big and dark brown. They match his curly hair.

Benny nods toward the empty chair at his table.

I glance at the name tag, checking to make sure it says Sarah Weber, and then I slide into the seat next to him. I've never noticed just how tall he is until now.

I unzip my backpack and shuffle my books, looking for my health notebook. Once I have what I need, I cross my legs and pull on my top, trying to get comfortable.

"Is that good?" Benny points to *The Clocks*, which is sticking out of my backpack.

"I'm not sure yet. The mystery might be easy to solve, and I really hate that. But I could be wrong."

"I only read graphic novels, but detective books are cool. I want to read a graphic novel about a detective."

"Um, yeah, me too," I say.

"I'll let you know if I find one."

"Okay. Thanks." I try to act like I'm not freaking out inside, when really I'm like—OMG! Benny is going to think about me when I'm not sitting in the same room as him and tell me if he finds a book I might like!

Coach Lemon claps to get our attention. She pushes her hair back behind her shoulders. It's so blonde, it's almost white. She waits until everyone stops talking before she starts. "The person you've been assigned to sit next to will be your partner for the next few weeks."

"Sup, partner," Benny whispers to me.

"Sup." I do everything I can to not smile, but I can't stop it from happening.

Benny and I aren't friends. Not really. We don't ignore each other in the hall or anything like that. We usually say "hey" or "what's up." But we've never been in the same class or had a reason to talk until now.

"Food is how we fuel our bodies and brains. We need different nutrients and vitamins to thrive and not get sick." Coach Lemon picks a stack of papers off the desk. "Today, we're going to look at different nutrition plans that are based on factors like age, height, weight, and physical activity level. Many of you are still growing, which means at times you might need more energy and food than I do, since I'm an adult and I'm done growing."

Duke says something under his breath.

Tamar covers her mouth, like she's trying not to laugh.

I'm not sure if Coach Lemon doesn't notice or if she just

doesn't care that they're talking about her. I don't need to hear what Duke said to know he's making a joke about Coach Lemon's height. She's tall, like really tall—six feet, two inches. She played forward at UConn and was going to the WNBA, but she got injured her senior year and needed ankle surgery.

"I'd like you to start by working with your partner on this assignment." Coach Lemon holds up the packets. "Please take one and pass it on."

Benny and I both read the directions, and then he says, "So, we just have to write down what we ate for dinner yesterday and the day before, and then put the different foods into nutrient groups, like protein, minerals, or vitamins, and write down the benefits of each one. Am I missing something? This seems way too easy."

"Maybe for you," I say before I realize what I'm doing.

"What do you mean?" he asks.

"Nothing." I stare at my sneakers.

"Last night, we had ash e reshteh, which is noodle soup. I made it, so I know all the ingredients."

"I didn't know you cooked." As soon as the words are out of my mouth, I wish I could take them back, because obviously I didn't know that. How would I know that?

"Yeah. I guess I, um, like trying new foods. I get kind of bored with eating the same meals too much, so it's fun for me to experiment and, like, test out different recipes. It's like an adventure."

"That's really cool," I say. I've never thought about cooking that way.

He smiles. "What did you have for dinner?"

"Scrambled eggs."

"Awesome. I wish my parents would make scrambled eggs for dinner. Or let me make them with butter and chives and"—he pauses, like he's thinking—"goat cheese. That would be so good."

I want to tell him that it's not awesome and that my eggs were plain and dry, but I don't say that out loud.

"Okay. What about the night before?"

I bite my lip. "Salmon and broccoli with lemon."

"With oil or butter? And what seasoning?"

I shrug. "I don't think either or any."

His eyes go wide. "Really?"

"My parents don't cook." I hunch my shoulders, wanting to disappear, because I don't know what's wrong with me that I didn't pretend, like always, like I do with everyone else, even my best friends. I could have picked oil and made up a few

34

spices or said I didn't remember, and he never would have known the difference.

"They have free cooking classes at the community center every week. Your parents should check them out."

"Maybe my dad would go. But my mom—" I shake my head. "She likes being a bad cook." My voice is so soft I can barely hear myself talking. "She thinks cooking isn't healthy or something."

"What? That doesn't even make sense. She's definitely wrong." Benny sounds annoyed, like it's personal to him, but I'm not sure why. "Just because you eat and cook well doesn't mean you're not healthy. Chef Emily Ying runs marathons. You should tell your mom that."

"Yeah," I say, because even though I would never say that to Mom, I don't think I should disagree with him or he'll think there's something wrong with me too. "Don't tell anyone, okay?"

"I won't." He looks at me, like he really means it, and I'm not sure why, but I believe him. "Don't sweat the assignment. I know how to make really good salmon and broccoli. I'll just add a few extra ingredients and then no one will know."

"Thanks."

"No big deal," he says.

But it is to me.

When we're finished writing everything down, Benny and I put the foods into categories. And even though I should feel weird that Benny knows this big embarrassing thing about me, I don't.

After school, Ryan and I snack on a giant bag of chips she brought from home, then change for practice and head out onto the court. As soon as I hear the ball pounding the wood floor and sneakers chirping, I'm in the zone.

We warm up with a half-court, three-man weave. I pass the ball to Emilia on my right and then run behind her as fast as I can toward the hoop, while she throws the ball to Tamar on the left. Tamar passes back to me, and I shoot a layup. Tamar, Emilia, and I run back to the other end of the court. I'm not thinking too much about getting everything right. I'm busy playing and having fun. All my hard work is there in my muscle memory. I know where my teammates are going to be without looking, and it feels good to be in sync. We keep weaving and shooting, until Coach Lemon blows her whistle and waves us over.

"We're working on conditioning today," Coach Lemon says.

"Ugh! Why?" someone says under their breath.

"I know these drills aren't the most exciting, but they're really important—basketball is running—so I expect you to give this practice everything you've got." She looks around the huddle, double-checking to be sure we understand how much this matters. "We're going to start on the baseline. When I blow the whistle, run to the free-throw line and back, then to half court and back, then to the far free-throw line and back, and then to the opposite baseline and back. We'll do that three times with a break in between each round. Then we'll split into two groups and do the same drill while dribbling the ball. If there's time, I'd like to end practice working on zone offense and defense. Let's get to it."

I stand on the baseline between Ryan and Emilia. We haven't even started running and I'm already out of breath, which is so not normal for me.

Ryan squeezes my hand. "Small wins," she whispers. It's kind of our BFF basketball motto.

"Small wins," I say, and squeeze back.

When the whistle blows, I run to the first free-throw line, bend down, tap the floor, and sprint back.

There isn't a lot of space between us, so I'm careful to stay in control of my arms and legs after I start to get tired and feel clumsy. I tap the floor, turn around, and run toward midcourt. My sneakers feel like they're filled with cement, dragging behind the rest of my body. I ignore the cramp in my right side and Ryan, who is running back toward me. It's not just Ryan. We've barely even started, and I'm already way behind almost everyone else on the team.

I push as hard as I can, but I don't know how to make my body move faster.

The other girls zip by me. I try to block them out. Only I can't. I don't cut corners or accidentally forget about the second free-throw line, even though part of me wants to and I'm pretty sure I won't get caught. But that's not the point. I keep running, even when everyone else is done and drinking water and I'm the only one left on the court.

The entire team is looking at me. I can feel their eyes, watching as I choke on air and try to finish.

We haven't run like this all season, and last year, I was always one of the fastest girls. I don't remember what it felt like to sprint before everything about me started to change. I guess maybe I didn't think so much when I was running back then. I wonder if all the thinking is slowing me down. I don't know how to make my brain go back to the way it was before, when I was fast and free and *never* the worst at anything in basketball.

Ryan and Emilia don't try to make me feel better between drills, probably because they know that's impossible. This isn't my first bad practice. Over the past five weeks, I've been getting worse. Not better. And it's not because I'm rusty. I changed. It's like every part of me is different, and now I'm slow and awkward, and that's not going away. The truth is— it doesn't matter that I'm the best shooter on the court if I can't move fast enough to get open.

I stay focused and push through practice. But I'm last in every drill by a lot.

When we're finally done for the day, we all huddle around Coach Lemon. She talks about staying hydrated and fueling our bodies. I stop listening, until I hear her say, "Great work! See you tomorrow." Then she walks over to me. "Let's chat for a minute," she says, and gestures for me to follow her away from the other girls.

Tamar and Sage are still standing around acting like they're talking about something important. I'm pretty sure they're trying to overhear whatever Coach Lemon is about to say to me. She waits until they give up and clear out of the gym before she starts talking, so it's obvious I'm right.

I don't look up at her. I already know she's disappointed in me, and I don't want to feel any worse than I already do. I keep my eyes on the floor.

She takes a deep breath, then sighs, like whatever is coming next is bad. "I don't want you to worry, Sarah. This has happened to a lot of girls I've coached. It happened to me my sophomore year. Your body is doing what it's supposed to do. It takes time to get used to the changes."

Coach Lemon noticed my body changing. She knows I've been getting slow. And she isn't worried. "How much time?" I ask. "Like a few weeks?"

"It's different for everyone," she says. "I know that's a frustrating answer."

"Can you guess? Or like give me an average or something?"

"I really don't know—"

"Please."

She sighs again. "I'd say a few months."

No! That's too long. We need to be in the Hall of Fame this year. "There has to be something I can do to get better now."

"Definitely," she says. "You can focus on developing new parts of your game. I promise you'll adjust and your body will feel like it's yours again soon."

I want to believe her. "You don't really know that, do you? There's no guarantee, right?"

She pauses like she's trying to figure out what to say next. "I know that some of what you're going through is temporary, like the feeling that you're out of breath all the time. And I'm confident you can become a more well-rounded player."

Well-rounded is like coach-code for average at everything. "So, for now I'm just bad at basketball." I feel my heart in my throat.

She shakes her head. "You're such a strong player, Sarah. Really. This is temporary. It's just puberty. Everyone goes through it."

"Then why does it feel like I'm the only one who's getting worse?"

"It doesn't make sense to compare yourself to other people. Everyone's body is changing at different times. And I want to make sure you understand that there's nothing wrong with your body just because it isn't doing the same thing as everyone else's."

I don't roll my eyes, because I like Coach Lemon and I don't want to be rude or disrespectful, but it really bothers me when adults say things that are obviously impossible and hypocritical. I mean, all they do is compare themselves to other people. Also it's, like, human nature, so I can't stop. And I'm pretty sure there is something wrong with my body, because it isn't working the way I need it to. I'm afraid that strong player she's talking about is gone, and she might never be back. It's like I got older and everything about me shifted around and part of me disappeared, and now I'm not sure who's left.

Coach Lemon pats me on the back. "Keep working hard. It'll be okay."

I want to ask how she knows, but I don't, because I'm pretty sure she's mostly guessing and hoping.

Dad is parked in front of the gym waiting for me when I get outside after practice.

"Hi, kiddo," he says as soon as I open the door and get in the car. He's smiling at me like it doesn't bother him that he's jet-lagged and tired because he's too tall to sleep on an airplane. He wanted to pick me up after work and see me. "Everything okay?"

I force a smile, but there are already tears in my eyes. And before I can stop everything I'm feeling from coming out, I'm crying.

Dad wraps his arms around me and holds on tight, like I'm little and he can still hug my problems away. "Rough day?"

I nod. "Practice was really bad."

"I'm sorry. I get it." And he usually does, since he used to be serious about basketball too. But this time, I don't think he'll understand, because I'm pretty sure basically everything is different for boys.

"I have good news."

I look up at him.

"Mom was too tired to cook, so I'm taking you out to eat."

I smile for real, because even though everything is bad, at least for tonight, I don't have to worry about dinner.

When we get to Sadie's, Dad and I sit at the counter and order burgers medium-well with cheddar cheese and extra special sauce. Neither of us says anything while we wait for our food. The silence feels weird and a little bad, like we're not just hungry and tired from our days, but like we're missing the piece that connects us.

If everything were different, we'd talk about the drills we ran in practice today or my next game, because basketball is the thing Dad and I have in common. He played in college. That's how he met Mom. Someone introduced them after one of his games. But right now even thinking about practice makes my heart hurt.

When our food is finally ready, neither of us waits to start eating.

"These burgers are my favorite," Dad says.

"Same," I say. "I have no idea why, but they're actually perfect."

"I can tell you—it's not the special sauce."

"How do you know?" I ask.

He nods toward the chef behind the counter who's combining ketchup and BBQ sauce and pouring the mixture into bottles that say *special sauce*.

"Maybe that's exactly why they're so good."

"Boom." Dad puts out his fist and bumps his against mine.

We eat for a little while, until we're both finished with our burgers.

I like eating with Dad. I never feel like he's watching me, and he never comments on other people's food unless he wants a bite. But he travels a lot for his job and he's out late most nights with clients. We don't get to have that many meals together. I love it when we do. He makes food easy and fun.

Dad leaves the grocery shopping to Mom during the week, and he's in charge of buying food on weekends. On Saturdays he goes to Provini and picks up eggplant Parmesan, Italian subs, rotisserie chicken, macaroni salad, homemade pretzels, and lemon poppy cake to fill our shelves. When he shows up with too many bags to carry from the car in one trip, I feel like everything is going to be okay, but then the food is gone, and I'm even more afraid that we'll never have that much to eat in our house again.

"Can you get some snacks for me when you go to the store?" I ask. "Like a few bags of chips?"

"Of course," he says.

"I made a list for Mom before my friends slept over. But she didn't follow it at all. She just got the same four things she always gets, plus one bag of Doritos."

"I'm sorry," he says. "Give me the list next time, okay? I'll make sure you have everything you need. I got you on this, because, you know, food is hard for Mom."

I hesitate. "Yeah. Okay," I say. "Thanks."

He nods. "No problem."

Only it is. But I'm not sure how to explain that food being hard for Mom is hard for me too. It feels like there are cracks inside me that no one else can see. Not even Dad.

By the time we get home, Mom is already in bed. The trash bag under the sink is filled with Hershey's wrappers, too many to count. This is a thing she does sometimes. She accidentally eats a lot of candy or cookies or both, and then she doesn't want to think about food for the rest of the day.

I wonder if Dad knows what really happened or if I'm the only one who notices.

I shower quickly, change, and start my homework, because I have a lot and it's already late. I finish English and history, and I'm about to start math when my phone buzzes. It's a group text from Ryan to Emilia and me: **Okay, so you don't have to write back if you don't feel like it, but we know practice today was kind of the worst, and we're here for you if you need anything.**

That's from both of us, Emilia texts.

I get that Ryan and Emilia are trying to make me feel better, but now I feel even worse knowing they've been sitting around talking about me behind my back. Only I don't tell them that part, because I'm pretty sure they're doing their best and that means something. **Thanks.**

And obviously we're all three BFFs for life no matter what, Ryan texts. **It doesn't matter to us if you're not on the team anymore. We weren't besties because of basketball anyway.**

WHAT? **What do you mean? Do you think I should quit?**

Wait, you didn't quit? Emilia texts. **We thought that's why you were talking to Coach after practice.**

46

It's hard to breathe. **No! Who said that?**

Neither of them writes back. I really hope they're not texting each other, trying to figure out what they should say to me.

I'm not sure who said it first, Emilia texts.

You really thought I'd quit and not tell you?

It's Emilia again: **We thought Coach Lemon was making you quit.**

Suddenly I'm sweating. It's too hot in here. I pull off my sweatshirt, but that doesn't help. I don't know what's worse— that someone started a rumor Coach Lemon kicked me off the team or that Ryan and Emilia believed it.

Neither of them writes anything else for a few minutes. And I guess I'm glad they don't try to make this better, because nothing is going to fix how I feel.

I'm sorry, Ryan texts.

Me too, Emilia adds.

It's okay, I write, even though it's not, because none of this is their fault.

You're so good at basketball. It's Ryan. **Please stay on the team.**

I am, I write.

Phew, Emilia texts. **Wait, so what were you talking to Coach Lemon about then?**

I swallow and breathe. I've been trying so hard not to think about what Coach Lemon said to me, but right now I can feel everything I'm afraid of twisting around in my stomach. I'm not waiting a few months to be good at basketball again. I need to find a way to get back to how I was before. **Nothing major. Just an idea for a set play.**

That's cool, Emilia writes, like she believes me. **Not to change the subject to Benny.**

Aka your favorite subject, Ryan texts.

Shut it. Anyway, like I was saying, Benny and I were texting. And he asked me for your number, Sarah... for health. I gave it to him.

OMG! Benny has my number in his phone right this second! I really want him to text me. I wonder when Emilia and Benny started texting and if they text all the time and what they talk about. I hope they didn't talk about me quitting basketball. But I don't ask, because I don't want to talk about basketball anymore, or Benny.

You didn't tell me you were partners, Emilia texts.

I forgot, I write, which is obviously a lie. I was just hoping it would never come up, since the three of us don't always talk about everything that happens in school. For example, I don't know who either of their partners are in health. Also, I try to avoid bringing up Benny around Emilia, because I'm pretty sure as soon as she hears me say his name, she'll know how I feel about him. **We didn't get to pick. It was assigned.**

Oh yeah. Duh! Same. But still, you're so lucky.

I hate to end this conversation talking about Benny, but I need to sleep, Ryan texts.

Night, I text back.

Xo, Emilia writes.

When I open my math notebook to finish my homework, my stomach rumbles, which makes sense since Dad and I got back from dinner a few hours ago. Normally I'd try to find something else to eat, like the Swedish Fish in the hallway closet, because even though I don't love them, I don't hate them either. But I have to figure out how to get good at basketball again. And maybe eating candy when there's nothing else to eat is one of the things I'm doing wrong. I take out the packet from health class to see if there's anything in there that might help me.

I flip through the pages, looking for answers, until I get to a list of healthy foods and a nutrition chart. I slide my finger down to where it says "12 years old," and then across to "45–60 minutes of activity per day," because that's me. Under the chart, there are examples of healthy meals and snacks. I start reading through the breakfast ideas. But I'm confused, because not every twelve-year-old is the same. That's what Coach Lemon said. And if this is what twelve-year-olds like Ryan should be eating, then I should be eating less. Because Ryan is still the same as always, and I'm different now. I have to get back to how I used to feel in my body and play the way I did last season, before I slowed down and stopped being able to perform, and I'm pretty sure that means eating less than a person like Ryan.

I never thought a lot about how much I was eating before, except when I was hungry and we didn't have food in the house, but right now eating less seems like the only way to get back to how I used to be. And even though the idea feels a little weird to me, so does being in my body right now. When I think about it that way, changing how I eat actually makes sense, because Coach Lemon said adults don't always need as much food as growing kids. It sort of feels like I'm more of an adult now.

I fill up my water bottle and drink as much as I can to try and make the hunger rumbles go away while I finish my homework. When I'm done, I take out *The Clocks*. It helps to get lost in someone else's problems for a while. I read and read and ignore the hungry feeling in the pit of my stomach—for basketball.

THREE

IN THE MORNING, I wake up early to practice sprints and free throws before school. I should be hungry. I was hungry last night when I went to bed, but at some point the empty feeling in my stomach disappeared.

I shower and drink a bottle of water while I change my clothes, put on mascara, blush, and lip gloss. I pick out a long-sleeved chambray dress with high-waisted tights. I get why some people hate tights, but they make me feel secure.

I run a brush through my still wet, frizzy brown waves, and hurry downstairs to the kitchen.

Dad must have had an early meeting because I heard the garage door open and close right after my alarm went off, and now Mom is sitting by herself at the table, dressed up for work. She's wearing a blue-and-coral paisley scarf that makes her shine even more than usual.

"Morning." She looks up from her book. "How did you sleep?"

"Fine." I drop my backpack and open the fridge. There are three plain, nonfat yogurts on the top shelf. Yogurt is on Coach Lemon's list. I take a container, grab a spoon from the drawer, and sit across from Mom.

The yogurt is sour and bland, but also good in a weird way, and the more I eat, the more I think I like the way it tastes.

"I didn't know you liked plain yogurt," Mom says.

"Me neither. I don't think I've ever had this kind before, but Coach Lemon gave us a list of healthy foods in class and plain yogurt was one of them."

"That's great, sweetheart. I'm so glad to hear you're trying to be healthy." Mom's voice is happy and maybe a little relieved.

"I was wondering if you could get some other things on the list when you go shopping?" I unzip my bag, find the packet from class, and hand the paper to her.

Mom scans the page, and after a few minutes, she says,

"Hmm. You were taught that these are healthy foods in school?"

"Yeah," I say.

Her eyebrows pinch. "I can buy some more yogurt, and they should have fresh apples today and cantaloupe and eggs. We're having lemon chicken and spinach for dinner. But I'm not so sure about this list, honey."

"Why not?" I ask.

"Some of the fruit on here has a lot of sugar. You don't want to eat too many bananas. They're starchy. And mangoes." She shakes her head. "They're more like candy."

"I didn't know that." I think about reminding her how much actual candy we have around the house, but I don't. "What about hummus and veggies?"

"Do you like hummus?" she asks.

I nod. "I had a garlic kind at Ryan's house. It was really good."

"I can get garlic hummus."

"Wait—is hummus bad for you?" I ask, because now I'm not really sure I can trust Coach Lemon's list. Not one hundred percent. I don't want to be like Mom, but she does know a lot about being healthy. She's read so many books on nutrition and exercise. There are like twenty in her office.

"It's made from chickpeas. It's very good for you in moderation."

"What do you mean?"

"It wouldn't be great to eat the whole container in one sitting."

"Got it," I say, even though that's exactly what Ryan and I did with a bag of pretzels. And now I'm totally confused about how to be healthy, since apparently even foods that are good for you can be starchy and sweet and bad for you too.

As soon as I get to school, the bell rings, which is great news for me, because even though I know eventually I'm going to have to face my teammates, I'd rather go straight to class and avoid talking to them for as long as possible.

The best part about drinking a lot of water is I sort of feel less hungry, and the worst part is I always have to go to the bathroom. But I manage to only go one time per class. I'm afraid that someone who is in all the same classes as me, aka Sage, is going to call me out on how often I ask to be excused, but it's important to be hydrated. Coach Lemon even said. Plus, I like that I can drink as much water as I want without worrying it will set me back in basketball.

By lunch, my stomach feels hollow. I want to sprint across

the courtyard into the cafeteria, cut the line, and eat everything in sight, but I don't.

Emilia is already sitting with Tamar and Sage. I look around, hoping Ryan is randomly at a different table, but I don't see her.

I pick a green apple and a turkey sandwich with lettuce and tomato on whole wheat bread, which is different for me. I usually get the hot lunch or pizza. I want to take another piece of fruit for later, in case I'm hungry before practice, but the only options, other than apples, are bananas and oranges, and I can't remember if oranges are a fruit like candy with lots of sugar or if they're okay or maybe Mom didn't say, so I get another apple, because apples feel safe and approved.

When I turn around, Benny is standing in front of me. He smells minty, and I wonder what it would be like to kiss him. It's not the first time I've thought about it, but now there's nothing I can do to stop. I really hope he can't tell.

"You didn't write back," he says.

"To what?" I ask.

"Um, my text."

"You didn't text me."

"I did," he says, and then recites my number.

Whoa! Benny memorized my number! Only the last

two digits are in the wrong order. "It's two five, not five two."

"Oh. Shoot. My bad."

"Do you memorize everyone's number?" The question is out of my mouth before I can think through what I'm saying and stop myself.

"Not everyone's," he says. "But I'm good at remembering things."

"Apparently not that good." I smile.

"Hold up." He looks at Ms. Chen, who's monitoring the cafeteria, fumbles around in his pocket, takes out his phone, and scrolls, like he's searching for something important. "I knew it. Emilia mixed up the numbers. She sent me the wrong one." He shows me his phone to prove it.

My mouth goes dry. I clear my throat. "Oops." I do my best to act like the mix-up doesn't mean anything and ignore the icky feeling in my stomach. Emilia was probably typing really fast. She does that sometimes. She wouldn't have given Benny the wrong number on purpose, especially since he told her he was asking for class. No way. We're best friends. It was definitely a mistake. "So, what did you say in your text?"

"I sent a pic of my dinner. I made tahdig."

"I've never had that. What's in it?"

"Crunchy fried rice with saffron." He looks around the cafeteria again, and then shows me.

I lean in closer to him. My stomach flips. "Wow. That looks so good."

"Thanks." He grins. "It was the best batch I've ever made. Oh, and I said I haven't found a graphic novel with a detective. So far, just spies. But I'm on a mission now."

"I mean, spies are cool too."

"Totally." He nods. "I'll, um, text your real number later so you'll have mine for homework . . . or, you know, whatever."

I wish I could ask what he means by "whatever," because it seems like maybe he wants to talk about things other than school too, but I know I can't do that, so I say, "Cool," and act like getting a text from him is no big deal at all, even though that's exactly the opposite of how I feel.

"Later," he says, and walks away.

I slide one of my apples into the front pocket of my backpack, then I look for Ryan, but she still isn't here, which is totally not like her. Even though I'd rather sit by myself or with literally anyone else, I walk over to Emilia and the girls from the team, because I don't want them to think I'm mad about the rumor. I need to act like I'm over it or they'll know

I'm not and everything will keep getting worse for me, because that's how this kind of thing works.

There isn't room next to Emilia at the table. I sit across from her in an empty chair between Sage and Ines.

"Where have you been?" Sage asks. "It's like you quit the team and went MIA."

"I didn't quit." I try not to sound mad, but I can't help it.

"I already told you that," Emilia says to Sage, and as soon as she does, I feel bad for thinking she gave Benny the wrong number on purpose, even for a second.

"Oh yeah. Duh. I don't know why I keep forgetting." She laughs a little to herself.

Before I can respond, Emilia cuts in and changes the subject to the dance next Friday, like she really has my back no matter what. Everyone forgets about me and starts talking about music.

If I'm being honest, I don't like dances. It's probably because I'm not confident about dancing to fast songs, and no one has ever asked me to dance during a slow song, so I'm not sure if I'm good at that either. Plus, the only person I want to dance with is Benny, and no one can know I like him, which means I can't ask him to dance or say yes if he asks me.

While everyone talks about the dance, I eat my sandwich.

My plan is to stop halfway through. Only before I realize, half the sandwich is gone. I take a few sips of water and give myself time to feel full, but even after I wait, I'm still hungry, so I take one more bite and then another. I know I didn't eat a lot and I definitely ate less than usual, but it feels like maybe I still ate too much. How do I even know what's too much and what's not enough?

After the bell, I get to the locker room early to change for practice in one of the stalls. I didn't use to care about privacy. But I do now.

When I walk out, Ryan is sitting by herself on the bench in front of her locker. She's wearing a sports bra and basketball shorts and holding a giant bag of Doritos. She's the same as always. I'm jealous that she still gets to be herself without even trying. I'd do anything to be the same way I used to be again.

I sit down next to her and slide my feet into my basketball sneakers. When I bend down to tie my laces, my sports bra digs into my ribs and pinches my shoulders. It doesn't fit right. None of mine do. They haven't for—I don't even know how long. But I keep forgetting how much they hurt until I'm dressed for practice. And I guess I haven't wanted to ask Mom for one more thing, when I'm constantly asking for food.

"Want some?" Ryan holds the bag of chips out in front of me.

I obviously do. Doritos are my favorite, and I swear they smell even more delicious and cheesy now that I'm not letting myself eat them. But I can't. I already ate more than half my sandwich at lunch. Plus, I'm only eating nutritious foods, and Doritos are definitely not on anyone's "healthy foods" list.

"I'm good," I say, and then bend down and start tying my laces.

"You're joking." Ryan waves the bag in my face.

"I just had a snack."

Her eyebrows shoot up. "You're the Dorito queen. That's why I brought the big bag."

"You're the best," I say, because I know Ryan is trying to be nice. She has no clue she's taunting me. "I just ate too many on Friday, and I don't want to get sick of them, you know?"

She shoves the bag into her locker and slams the door shut. "Um, no. Not really."

I wish I could tell her what I'm thinking—that I hate my body and it's getting in the way of everything I want, and I'm never going to eat Doritos ever again, because eating too much and eating bad things is the reason my body is different. And my body being different now is why I keep messing up in basketball. But I can't say any of that to Ryan, because she won't understand. She's the same as always. Nothing about her has changed. She has no idea what this feels like.

When practice starts, Coach Lemon splits us into groups of five to work on offensive plays. We have to pass three times before anyone can even try to shoot.

I'm standing to the left of the basket, attempting to get open and away from Sage, who's guarding me. Every time I pivot or slide or move, my chest bounces and hurts.

I cut in, sprint out, get open. Emilia passes the ball to me. I know I've only been eating less for one day and I get that Sage isn't trying that hard, because I saw her roll her eyes at Tamar when Coach Lemon paired us up. But even still, I swear I feel a little lighter on my feet. I dribble left, then between my legs and back to the right, faking out Sage, and pass to Ryan, like I own the court, because I want everyone watching to remember I'm good at this part.

Ryan shoots and scores! Then she runs over to me.

We high-five, low-five, pivot-turn, and fist-bump, and for a few seconds, I feel like myself again, and like maybe my plan is going to work.

On the ride home with Mom, I'm jittery. I can't stop

tapping my feet, like I drank soda and now there's caffeine and sugar pumping through me. Only I obviously didn't, because soda is filled with chemicals and calories. It's worse than Doritos.

"How was practice?" Mom asks.

"Pretty good," I say. Usually I turn up the radio right about now, but I have to talk to Mom. I clear my throat and force words out. "It hurts when I run. I need a different sports bra. I'm sorry. I know we just got new ones, but they don't fit."

"Sarah, honey, please don't apologize." Mom stops the car at a red light and reaches for my hand. "I don't want you to be in pain." She glances at the clock. "I'd take you to the store now, but I have a work call."

"That's okay," I say. "It can wait."

"No, it can't," she says. "You have a game tomorrow. I can go to the store in the morning and pick out a few different options. I'll drop them off at school during lunch. Just don't forget to keep the tags on the ones you want me to return."

I smile. "I won't. Thanks, Mom." I love how she gets that every game is important without me having to explain. Mom never played basketball, but she loves to watch. Grandpa used to take her to Celtics games, so she knows a lot about hoops. And she takes my basketball seriously, like it really matters.

"You're welcome," she says. "I'm so glad you told me."

"Me too." It feels good that Mom can help me with something for basketball.

When we pull into the garage, Dad's car is parked in the other spot, and he's waiting for us in the kitchen. He hugs me and then kisses Mom.

"What are you doing home?" she asks.

"My meeting was canceled."

"Lucky us!"

"How was practice?" Dad asks me.

"Better than yesterday." I open the fridge. There are three more plain yogurts, hummus, and a container of celery and carrots.

"I'm glad," he says. "But not surprised."

"They didn't have the good apples," Mom says to me, before I have a chance to notice. "I got pears." She points to the two pieces of fruit on the counter.

"Thanks!" I say, trying not to seem shocked, even though I am. I can't believe she followed my list and even picked out replacement fruit for the apples, so now I know pears are approved. "Can you check again tomorrow?"

"Sure," she says, like food is always this easy, and all I have to do is ask for what I want and I'll get it. It turns out Mom does know how to buy food for me when it's healthy and on her list.

After Mom's call, we sit down for dinner, which doesn't happen very often, because Dad travels for work and Mom sometimes has classes or meetings at night.

We serve ourselves—chicken and spinach with garlic—passing the plates around the table. Once everyone has food, Dad and I start eating. I finish my spinach first. Then I cut my chicken in half and then in half again. I eat one piece at a time. It's bland and rubbery, but tonight I don't mind. I like knowing that Mom didn't use anything other than cooking spray, pepper, and lemon to make the food.

Mom cuts up her chicken. Every now and then, she takes a bite, but she's not actually interested in eating what she made. She never is. I wonder if Dad notices that Mom avoids eating, or if it's the type of thing that happens so often it doesn't register.

"Guess what, Sarah," Mom says. "I was reading *The Mirror* between classes, and I ran into the head of the English department. We started talking about how much we love mysteries, and she asked if I'd want to teach a class on detective novels in the fall."

"OMG!" I drop my fork, and it clinks against the plate. "You said yes, right?"

Mom nods. Her eyes are happy and nervous at the same time. "The class still needs to be approved, but if it is, it's mine!"

"Liv, that's incredible," Dad says.

"Fingers crossed." I hold both my hands in the air to show her.

"Thanks. If this happens, I'll need to turn around a syllabus pretty quickly. I could use your help." Mom is waiting to know what I think, and I want to scream—*Yes!* But the way she's looking at me right now makes me feel so close to her and I don't want this moment to end. "So, what do you think?"

"Duh!" I say. "I mean, obvs! It's our thing."

"Yeah. It is." She smiles. "I was actually thinking about having the class read two novels at once the way we do. I'd pair authors from different time periods where the detectives are solving the same type of mystery."

"That's seriously so cool!"

I take one more bite of chicken and leave the last piece on my plate, because even though I'm not full, I'm not hungry either, and I think that's the right place to stop.

After I help clean up dinner, I finish my homework and

get into bed with *The Clocks*. I think I love detective stories the most because it's fun to imagine I'm the person in charge of finding out the answers to important questions. Detectives aren't exactly superheroes. But they know how to pay attention to details, follow their instincts, and listen to themselves. I wish I could be more like that—like a person who knows I'm right, even when no one else agrees.

FOUR

WHEN I WAKE UP, my stomach sounds loud, like the garbage disposal, gurgling and bubbling and churning up nothing. I'm pretty sure I could eat everything in our house, including but not limited to all the yogurts in the fridge, the Swedish Fish in the hallway closet, the broken granola bar at the bottom of my backpack, and the entire bag of chocolate chip cookies Mom keeps in the freezer. But we have a game after school, and I don't want to give up now. I didn't blow it in practice yesterday. All I need to do is stay focused and stick to the plan.

I look at my phone. Benny still hasn't texted me. He probably forgot. Maybe he's been busy texting Emilia. The minute the thought enters my mind, I wish it hadn't. I don't want to compete with my best friend for a boy.

When I get downstairs, Mom is sitting at the kitchen table drinking coffee and reviewing her notes for class.

"Morning," I say.

"Good morning." Her eyes follow me as I take a yogurt from the fridge. "You look nice today. I love turquoise on you."

I pull at my sweater. "Thanks." Everything good about me is temporary and could just vanish. I take out my book so I have something to hide behind.

"Did you read ahead?" Mom asks.

"Uh, yeah, but only a little. I mean, I tried to stop but Poirot just—"

"Don't say it!" She cuts me off.

I cover my mouth. "Oops!"

We both laugh.

I taste a spoonful of yogurt. It's sour, and my lips pucker.

"You should add cinnamon," Mom says. Only before I can respond, she gets the glass jar from the spice rack and puts it on the table in front of me, like she's afraid if she doesn't act fast, I might go back to eating cereal for breakfast.

I take another bite. "I don't like cinnamon."

"Really?" She sounds confused. But she shouldn't be. It's the kind of thing she should remember because I say it a lot. "Cinnamon is good for your metabolism. It helps speed things up."

"I know," I say softly, because Mom has told me that so many times. Only it doesn't matter how strong her arguments are for eating cinnamon. They can't change the fact that I don't like the flavor. And I'm not going to eat things that taste bad to me.

Mom sighs. "Sarah, honey, I found out this morning that I have a meeting during your game."

"What?" The question falls out of my mouth and crashes onto the floor.

"I know." She rubs my shoulder.

"You can't get out of it?" I ask.

Mom shakes her head. "I tried. I'm so sorry."

I swallow hard. I know it shouldn't matter. It's not Mom's fault she can't be there. But she's never missed one of my games. And this feels like another thing that's different.

"You know how much I love watching you play. If there were anything I could do to get out of this, I would."

I nod, because I know that's true.

"I won't forget the bras. And Ryan's mom is going to drive

you home after." She wraps her arms around me, and I hug her back. "You'll be great." Her breath is warm against my ear. "You're always amazing. You're my star."

I hold on a little tighter, trying to soak in every last drop of love.

School goes by fast. And even though I woke up hungry, I manage to have a good eating day. For lunch, I have an apple and half a turkey sandwich again, which gives me this feeling like I can do anything. I'm in charge of what happens to me. It's weird how eating less makes me feel so much stronger.

Before the game, I stop by the office and pick up the tote bag Mom left for me. I wait until I'm in the stall with the door locked behind me before I look inside. There are three new bras, and they're all really cute. There's a hot-pink racerback, a neon-blue pullover, and one with a purple-and-black design. I can tell Mom tried hard to pick colors and styles she thought I'd like.

The blue bra is a little tight, but I try to get my arms through anyway, because I looked at the size and it's much bigger than my old bras, so it should fit. Only when I hear the seam start to pull, I stop. The pink one is a different brand, but a smaller size than the bra I couldn't get over my head. I almost don't bother trying it on. But I'm glad I do, because it's perfect. Weird. I jump up and down and run in place. My chest still bounces a little, but a lot less than before, and it doesn't hurt. I get that the design shouldn't be important to me, because I'm a serious b-ball player, but I like how the bra looks kind of fashion-y. It's like Mom knew exactly what I would want. And now needing a new bra doesn't even feel bad.

By the time I step onto the court, I'm ready to win.

While we warm up, I keep looking over at Coach Lemon, but she's watching the girls on the other team, who are zipping around their side of the court, like they have motors or magic.

When the buzzer goes off, we circle up. I stand sandwiched between Ryan and Emilia in the huddle. Coach Lemon talks about teamwork. She sounds excited and nervous and ready too. "This is a very athletic team. I'm sure you've noticed they have some impressive players. They're fast. But if we play as a cohesive unit, work hard, and communicate, we'll come out ahead," she says. "Let's start in zone, but extend to cover the three-point line and try to disrupt their shooting rhythm. I want to hear a lot of talking out there, especially on defense. We're not taking big risks in the first quarter. We need to stick together to make this win happen."

I stare at the shiny hardwood floor and try to stay calm, which is impossible since Coach Lemon just said she doesn't want to take any chances. Right now, it doesn't matter that I'm a starting forward; I'm also the least reliable player on the team.

"I'd like Ines to start at center. For guards, let's go with Ryan and Emilia." Coach pauses and glances at her notes, then looks back up and scans the huddle. "Our forwards will be Tamar and—" She looks around again and stops when she sees me, like she's taking back what she just said about risks and picking me anyway, because deep down she knows I can help us win.

I hold my breath.

"—Sage."

My throat closes up. It doesn't matter that I knew this might happen. It hurts to be demoted.

Coach Lemon says, "Hands in."

We all reach into the middle of the circle.

"Go team!" My voice is loud and hopeful mixed in with everyone else's.

The starters run to center court. It's weird to watch from

the sidelines and to know Mom isn't in the stands, but I focus on the game and cheer for my teammates, because I need to be ready to play my best when Coach Lemon decides to put me in. I sit as close as I can to where she's standing, because I want to be the first person she sees when she looks over here.

I keep waiting for her to say Sarah, but every time she turns to the bench, looking to sub one of the players, her eyes pass by me, and she calls another name. After halftime, I can feel myself start to sink deeper into the bench. I'm afraid if I stay here for too long, I might disappear.

We're up by ten points with four minutes left in the game before she has me switch places with Sage. I run out onto the court. And for the first time all season, my chest doesn't hurt. I'm not in any pain. I push myself to get open. Only I can't move fast enough. It doesn't matter that I know exactly where I need to be and how to get there, I can't make it happen. No one passes to me. I don't touch the ball or have a chance to do anything important before the buzzer goes off at the end of the game.

We won. I should be happy and hugging my teammates, because we're having an amazing season. But this victory doesn't belong to me. I barely played. Ryan is on the other end of the court with Emilia. She isn't looking around for me to celebrate. It feels like I'm not even here. I don't matter at all.

After I shake hands with the other team and say *good game* on repeat, Ryan and I grab our bags from the locker room, walk outside to the parking lot, and slide into the Martins' minivan. Mrs. Martin stands next to the car on the driver's side, talking to one of the other basketball moms about the boys and their scholarship options.

Ryan sighs and buckles her seat belt. "Sorry." She nods in her mom's direction.

"No biggie," I say, because I don't want Ryan to apologize to me when I know listening to her mom go on and on about her brothers is hard enough for her. It doesn't matter how well she plays or how big our team wins. It can't ever just be about her, because they're older and they're boys, and even though it's not fair that their dreams and games matter more, in her family they do, and I know nothing I say is going to make Ryan feel better. I've tried all the ways.

"Are you okay?" Ryan asks.

I shrug, because I'm not and I don't want to lie to her, but I don't want to talk either.

"I get that it feels bad, but—"

"You don't," I say back. Ryan has never sat on the bench for more than a few minutes to catch her breath or give other girls on the team a chance to play when we're winning by a lot. I hadn't either until today, so I know for sure she doesn't get how bad I felt watching and waiting to be picked and wishing I could make myself disappear, because I already felt invisible and worthless.

"Don't give up. We need you." Her voice is strained, like she's the one who's desperate for me to get better.

"Not really," I say. "You won without me."

"We need points if we're going to make the Hall of Fame and that has to happen." She looks right at me. "You're our best scorer."

"Then why didn't Coach put me in? I thought I played better in practice yesterday."

"You did. I swear. She's probably just giving you a little extra time to get your confidence back."

"Yeah," I say. "I guess." Because that could be true.

"It's going to be fine. You believe me, right?"

"Always." I trust Ryan. She would never lie to me about basketball. It's way too important to her.

Her mom opens the car door and gets into the front seat. "There are waters and snacks up here, girls." She hands Ryan

75

a bag of food, then slips on her glasses and looks at herself in the mirror in the same way Ryan does, like she's checking to make sure she didn't forget anything.

"Thanks," Ryan and I both say at the same time.

I twist open a water. I'm not thirsty, but I need to stall. I can't eat chips or Cheetos or cheesy crackers. I didn't exercise, unless you count four minutes on the court where I never broke a sweat, which I don't.

Ryan tosses me Cheetos. Then she opens her own bag and starts eating. She doesn't say anything, but she's looking at me, and I feel like I can't say no again, like I did with the Doritos, or she'll figure out that I'm being different about food.

I put an orange puff in my mouth. It's salty and bad for me and not on the list.

By the time we pull into my driveway, I've eaten one, two, three crunchy pieces.

"Thanks for the ride," I say to Mrs. Martin.

"Great game." She turns around to face me. I can't tell if she's trying to be nice by acting like it doesn't matter that I barely played because everyone on the team is important or if she wasn't watching. But by the way she's smiling, I'm pretty sure she has no clue how bad the game was for me.

I grab my bags and my Cheetos, get out of the car, and shut the door. Then I walk as fast as I can until I'm inside my house. It's dark. My parents aren't home from work yet, and I'm not sure if I feel relieved that no one is here to ask me about the game or even worse now that I'm alone.

I turn on the light in the kitchen, and put the Cheetos in the trash.

I look to see what Mom left for dinner. There's usually a baking dish wrapped in foil waiting for me. But there's nothing on the stove. I'd be fine with rubbery chicken or leftovers or anything on the good list. I open the oven. It's empty. So is the fridge. And the freezer, except for the bag of cookies.

Mom forgot about dinner—about me.

I feel a hot rush of tears behind my eyes. I squeeze them shut, trying to stop myself from crying, but it's too late.

This happens a lot. All the time, actually. It's been like this for as long as I can remember. Mom forgets about food, especially after I ask for something specific. It's like talking about food means there will be even less to eat. I know it shouldn't bother me. I'm trying to eat less anyway. But it's worse now that I'm not full from snacking on chips. There's nothing to protect me from feeling how much it hurts that I'm not important enough for Mom to remember to feed me.

I guess I was hoping this wouldn't happen again, because she bought me all that healthy food when I gave her the list, but now it's mostly gone. I shouldn't have to remind Mom that I need to eat.

I take out the carrots and celery and then measure two tablespoons of hummus because that's the serving size on the back of the container and I don't want to accidentally eat too much, since Mom said hummus is only okay in moderation. I put the last yogurt into a bowl and cut up the last pear, even though that means there will be nothing to eat for breakfast tomorrow.

My phone is humming in my jacket. I'm sure it's Emilia checking in on me, and I'd rather ignore her, but I don't. I look at the message, because I think it's probably better to know what everyone is saying than to sit here imagining the worst. Only the text isn't from Emilia or Ryan or anyone on the team.

It's Benny. My heart speeds up. He didn't forget!

Hey, I text back.

He doesn't say anything for a few minutes, and I wonder if maybe I'm supposed to ask him a question. I've never texted a boy before, so I don't know the rules about what to say and how to say it.

I wish I could ask Emilia for advice, because she knows everything about boys and how to act around them. She had a really serious boyfriend before she moved here. They kissed. A lot. Like all the time. She's practically an expert compared to me, since I've never even had a boy like me back. Only I can't ask her to help, because it's Benny—and she likes him too.

A minute later, my phone finally buzzes again. **Sorry about the game.**

What do you mean? We won.

I know. But you didn't play.

My chest tightens. **Who told you that?** I need to know that it wasn't one of my teammates.

Duke. He was there.

I take a breath.

He adds, **I get it. Being benched is the worst.**

You've been benched before?

Yup. I guess my head hasn't really been in the game.

Sorry, I write. **And thanks. It helps that I'm not the only one. It's been a bad day.**

What else happened?

The last time Mom forgot dinner, I didn't tell anyone. Not Dad or Emilia or Ryan. But it was different, because we'd had a party in French class during last period with croissants and macarons and Brie. I wasn't hungry when I got home or by dinnertime. And even though I want to pretend I'm totally fine, I'm hungry, and there's a weight on top of me, pressing down on my shoulders and chest. And I want someone to know what happened, so it's real. **My mom forgot dinner. She's working late. And my dad is away tonight.**

Are you serious? I mean, I know you are. But I don't get it.

Me neither. I'm not sure what I did wrong or how to make this never happen again.

Your parents can't forget to feed you. That's like part of their job.

I know. It only happens sometimes, I text. **Not like every night or anything.**

It's happened before? Not okay. You need to eat.

I did. I don't tell Benny what I had, because he probably won't think I ate enough. I should be thankful no one is making me eat too much dinner.

I'm annoyed at your parents.

Ditto. Benny makes me feel like it's okay to be upset that there was nothing for dinner and that no one cares if I eat.

The garage door rumbles open. A few minutes later, there are footsteps on the stairs, and then a knock on my door.

"Come in," I say.

Mom walks into my room holding two chocolate chip cookies. "How was your game?" She sits down next to me on my bed.

"We won." I stare into my textbook.

She rubs my shoulder with her free hand. "That's great, sweetheart."

I shrug kind of hard, hoping she'll get the hint and move her hand, but she doesn't, so I inch away from her. "I didn't play, so it was good for the team. Bad for me."

"I don't understand. You're one of the best players."

"Guess not."

Mom puts her cookies on my desk, and then pulls me in close to her, like she wants to protect me from all the bad things that happened today. Only I don't want a hug. It's not helping. I want her to care if I eat.

Eventually she lets go and picks up her cookies.

I breathe in. This is my chance to say something. "There was nothing for dinner."

Mom covers her mouth. "I forgot." She shakes her head. "I can't believe I did that. I was so distracted by the meeting and my presentation. I'm sorry, Sarah."

I get that she wasn't trying to hurt me, but she did. And nothing she does or says right now is going to fix how empty and sad and forgotten I feel.

"Did you find something to eat?" she asks.

"We barely have any food," I snap.

"There's always pasta."

"It expired."

"Honey, spaghetti doesn't expire."

"Well, it did in September."

Mom sighs. "Want a cookie?" She holds one out to me.

"I don't like cookies."

She tilts her head. "Everyone likes cookies."

"I don't," I say it again, louder this time, because I want her to hear me.

She gives me a look, like she doesn't believe me. "That's impossible." Mom loves sweets and hates actual food so much she can't imagine anyone having a different opinion.

I guess I know by now that nothing I say is going to change how she is about food, but we don't have anything to eat for breakfast, and I don't want to wake up hungry and have to eat the old granola bar in my backpack that isn't on the list. So I need to at least try. I clear my throat. "We don't have any yogurts left—for tomorrow. And you said you were going to buy apples. But you didn't."

"I can go to the store in the morning before school," Mom says, tucking my hair behind my ears.

"Do you promise?"

"I promise," she says, so I'm sure she heard me.

I don't understand why sometimes she listens and I know I can count on her and other times it's like I'm not even there.

FIVE

AT SCHOOL, THERE'S a crowd of people by the door, waiting to sign up for Chef Junior auditions, because apparently *everyone* in our school knows how to cook.

I don't stop to see who's in line. It's not their fault they have parents who feed them and teach them life skills, and I don't.

When I finally make my way down the hall and over to Emilia and Ryan, they're too busy listening to something Tamar is saying about the dance to notice me. I should be relieved no one is talking about the game, but I'm standing behind my best friends, outside the group, and right now I feel like this is where I belong.

My stomach grumbles, which is weird, because I had a yogurt and an apple for breakfast, and that's more than I've been eating lately. I take a piece of sugar-free watermelon gum from my pocket, start chewing, then tap Ryan on the shoulder.

She inches over to make space for me, and Emilia scoots a little too. I slide into the circle with a bestie on each side.

"I'm wearing jeans and a spaghetti-strap tank top with sneakers," Tamar says in this way like we should all definitely care. "My hair is going to be down in loose curls per usual."

"I'm wearing sneakers too," Ryan says.

Tamar nods. "Casual is the new dressed up."

"Um, no," Emilia says. "The first dance of the year is major. I'm wearing a purple dress with little flowers and booties."

"Wow." Sage pulls on the end of her braid. "Bold."

"I like it. Be yourself," Tamar says to Emilia. "Now we just have to wait and see who's going to dance together!"

"Well, you and Duke," Sage says to Tamar. "Duh!"

Tamar shrugs. "TBD."

"Please," Emilia says. "He loves you."

Tamar grins, like she knows Emilia's right and there's no way she can jinx it. I can't imagine ever feeling that confident about anything. "You and Benny?" Tamar asks Emilia.

Emilia blushes and crosses her fingers on both hands. "He definitely acts like he wants to be BF-GF."

"It's happening," Tamar says. "He one hundred percent like-likes you."

My chest hurts.

"I hope you're right," Emilia says.

I hate that Emilia and I want the same thing. I'd rather be on her side and cross my fingers for her, but I'm a bad friend, because I don't want Benny to ask her to dance or ask her out. I wish I'd just told Emilia about my crush on Benny when she first told me about hers, before the fact that I like him turned into this secret and it was too late to tell her the truth.

"Who do you want to dance with?" Sage looks at me.

"No one," I say.

She rolls her eyes. "Mm-hmm."

"She's telling the truth." Emilia backs me up. "Sarah doesn't like anyone."

Sage smirks. "I bet."

The sugar-free watermelon flavor is gone. The bland

gum makes my stomach turn. I try to think of a way to prove I don't like him. Only before I can, the bell rings.

In health, Sage turns around and glares at me whenever Coach Lemon has her back to the class, like she wants me to know she's watching. I don't look at Benny once. Not even when he asks to borrow a pencil.

At the end of class, we're working on a short assignment about stress. We have to write about a time we experienced a fight-or-flight response. Coach Lemon didn't say we were going to have to share our work, but she didn't specifically say we wouldn't have to, so I write about a time I thought I lost my phone at a basketball tournament, just in case I have to read out loud in front of the class.

I've written a few sentences when Benny leans in and whispers, "You're going to the dance, right?"

"I guess."

"You don't seem super pumped."

I shrug. "I'm bad at dancing."

"I don't believe you." He adjusts his glasses.

"I wouldn't lie about being bad at something."

"I didn't say you were lying. You're probably just not dancing to the right music or like, um, with the right person." His eyes fall onto his notebook.

"Maybe." I try not to smile, but I can't stop, and I need to before Sage looks back at me and notices.

"I like dances," he says. "I'm into music. My older sister, Asha, and I listen to a lot of underground house. Or we used to. I guess she's not that into it anymore."

"That's really cool."

"Thanks." He smiles.

"I talked to my mom. I told her it wasn't okay that she forgot dinner."

"That's brave."

My stomach flips. "Thanks," I say. "It didn't actually help. She just said she was sorry and offered me a cookie."

"Your mom can't give you a cookie for dinner."

I don't get why Benny is so opinionated about food. It's weird. But I don't say that out loud. I say, "Yeah, I know," and then I look back down at my notebook and start writing again.

I finish just as the bell rings.

"Auditions for Chef Junior are three weeks from Saturday," Coach Lemon says. "There's no fee to enter. And I'll be giving out extra credit to anyone who participates. If you're interested, you can register in the lobby today or online for the rest of next week." She points to the website on the board.

"We should sign up," Benny says.

"Funny," I say.

"Not kidding. Come over this weekend. I'm like a professional chef. I swear." He's looking at me like he's totally serious. "I'll teach you how to cook. So, then it won't matter that your parents can't."

I want to say yes, and hang out with Benny alone and not have to worry about who's watching us. But I can't do that without telling Emilia.

"It'll be fun. And we'll get extra credit for class."

"You should be partners with Duke or one of your friends."

"Or not. I don't even want Duke to know I'm entering the contest. He thinks cooking is for girls or something stupid."

"That doesn't make sense," I say. "Most famous chefs are dudes."

"Exactly. So, you're in?"

"I'll try." The words fall out of my mouth. "But don't tell anyone, you know, just in case it turns out I'm really bad and you're too embarrassed to compete with me."

"Uh, that won't happen, but fine. Deal." Benny smiles at

me, like he's really happy, like maybe he needs this too. "I'll sign us up. Can you practice on Saturday at one?"

"Yeah," I say. "That should be good."

At lunch, I get my sandwich and apples from the cafeteria and go to the library before anyone sees me. I don't feel like talking about the dance or Emilia and Benny and how they're meant to be together forever. Also, I don't want to lie about Chef Junior. So, I need to avoid Emilia until I can explain why it's totally not sketchy that Benny and I entered a cooking competition together.

If anyone asks why I wasn't at lunch, my plan is to say that I didn't finish my French homework. I keep my head down and walk as fast as I can to the back of the library, far away from the glass windows, and over to fiction. I love hiding in the stacks between rows of books, like somehow the stories with their mystery and magic and unexpected plot twists can protect me from everything that's real.

In the back of my math notebook on a blank piece of graph paper, I write down what I think is going to happen so I can track my theories as they develop and keep a record of when I figure out the ending. *The Murder of Roger Ackroyd* is the only crime I couldn't solve before the detective, which is probably why that book is my favorite.

While I read *The Mirror*, I eat an apple and half my sandwich.

I'm so lost in the story that I almost don't hear the bell ring or care that I'm still hungry. All I want to do is keep reading and find out what's going to happen next and stay in this fictional world where I don't have to worry.

When I step onto the court for practice, I'm nervous. I stay focused and every drill goes by fast. I can still feel myself holding on a little too tight, like I'm trying to not mess up. But for once I don't have to adjust my bra. It makes me realize how much time I was spending rearranging myself.

At the end of practice, when Coach Lemon tells us we're going to run ladders for the last ten minutes, my heart starts racing.

I hear someone giggle.

But I don't look to see who it is. I breathe in, walk to the baseline, and wait for the whistle. Once we start running, I feel okay. I'm a little lighter on my feet. It's easier to push myself forward.

I'm not the first to finish. Not even close. But I'm not far behind everyone either. I'm faster than last week. I can keep up with the team. My speed is coming back.

We're all catching our breath when Coach Lemon dribbles the ball across the court and passes to Ryan. She doesn't have to say anything. We know how this works. Ryan has to shoot a free throw. If she makes the shot, practice is over. If she misses, we run again.

Everyone has their own free-throw ritual to relax and focus them. Ryan dribbles to the side—*thump, thump*—takes a breath and shoots. As soon as the ball is in the air, I know her shot is short. And I'm right—it barely hits the front rim.

"Ugh," Ryan mumbles.

I breathe, and get ready to run.

Coach Lemon blows the whistle.

I sprint, touch the line, and run back to where I started, pushing myself to keep pace with my teammates.

When we're back at the baseline, Coach Lemon hands the ball to Ines, who's next to Ryan. She's going down the line. So if Ines doesn't make this shot, I'm up.

I know shooting free throws at the end of practice after sprinting is hard for everyone, which is exactly why Coach Lemon has us practice this way. It simulates what happens in a game. The only time anyone ever has a chance to shoot a free throw, they're worn out from running. But I'm not too worried. Ines practices a lot.

She dribbles—one, two, three times—spins the ball—and shoots. The ball makes it to the hoop, circles the rim, falls to the side, and bounces away.

"Seriously?" Sage says under her breath, but loud enough for everyone standing around us to hear.

"So annoying," someone else grunts.

I don't turn to see who's huffing. I'm up next, and I need to be ready.

The whistle blows. I run.

The second I'm done, Coach Lemon passes the ball to me. I breathe, focus on the basket, and let my muscle memory do the work. I spin the ball—dribble, dribble—like always. It's my ritual. I'm about to shoot. But my head feels light and the hoop starts swaying. I'm dizzy. I close my eyes and breathe in. When I open them, everything is still and steady again. I start over. I'm in the zone. No one else exists. I spin the ball, *thump, thump,* shoot, and follow through.

It's going in. I can feel it. But I stand there watching, waiting, until—*swish.*

A few people cheer.

"That's it for today. Great work!" Coach Lemon grins at me.

"Woo-hoo! Go, Sarah!" Emilia shouts. She puts her arm over my shoulder and leans against me.

I smile for real, because I'm turning things around in basketball. All I have to do is stick to my plan and I can put everything right back to the way it was before.

SIX

ON FRIDAY, RYAN leaves school after second period, because she's going to North Carolina with her family on a college visit for her brothers. I take my lunch to the library, because I'm still avoiding one-on-one convos with Emilia. I don't know how to tell her that Benny and I are competing together in Chef Junior and that I'm going over to his house to practice cooking this weekend. I keep trying out different versions in my head, hoping to find a good way to explain myself, but there isn't one. So, I haven't said anything, which I'm pretty sure is worse. I'm going to have to tell her, before everyone finds out in three weeks at the audition.

When I see Emilia in the bathroom between classes, she

gives me a big hug, and then looks at herself in the mirror. "My lips are so chapped and, like, crusty."

"It's really dry in here." I pull a lip gloss from my pocket and hand it to her. It's new and a little brighter than I normally wear, but I like the way it makes me look.

She coats her lips and then turns to me. "What do you think?"

I nod. "Really good."

"Like Benny is going to want to be my boyfriend good?"

I should tell her now. We're alone. I could be totally cool and like whatever about the whole thing. Emilia is the person I count on to tell me the truth, and I want to be honest with her too. She deserves to know, and I'm pretty sure it would be easier to say everything than to act like I don't have secrets piling up when I do.

"Hello? Earth to Sarah?" Emilia waves a hand in front of my face. "Are you okay?" She looks worried.

"Yeah. Sorry," I say. "I'm just tired. You look so pretty."

"Thanks." She glances back at the mirror, untucks her hair from behind her ears, and looks at herself one final time, like she wants to make sure everything is still where she left it. "PS. You totally showed the haters who's boss at practice. Do you feel so good now? Because you should. You rocked."

"Yeah. I do." I want to ask her to name the specific haters she's talking about right now, but I guess I already know it's Sage and Tamar.

"I'm annoyed we can't hang tonight," she says. "I'd much rather be at your house than at some stupid old-person dinner in Boston." She rolls her eyes. "Boring."

I roll my eyes back. "I'm bummed." But really I'm thankful Emilia has plans tonight and I don't have to come up with an excuse for why she can't sleep over, because she can't, since (A) I'm going to Benny's on Saturday and (B) hangouts involve chips and cookies, and even if I asked Dad to buy both, I can't eat them. Not now.

On Saturday, it's noon by the time I wake up. Only it doesn't feel like I slept in. I'm still so tired. I'm pretty sure I could fall back asleep for the rest of the day. But I'm going to Benny's house to learn how to cook, so I have to get ready. I force myself out of bed and into the bathroom.

After I shower, I drink a bottle of cold water and try to get dressed. I don't feel good in my clothes. Everything is pulling and sticking and making me uncomfortable. I'm afraid that all the parts of me I don't want to change are still changing anyway, even though I'm eating less, which doesn't make sense. I had a perfect eating day yesterday, and the day before.

I bet it's the bread. It has to be. I've only been eating half my sandwich every day and it's whole wheat, which is on Coach Lemon's list, and sometimes Mom eats whole wheat bread. But I'm starting to wonder if maybe it's not okay for me to eat bread every day. Maybe it's one of the foods I can only have in moderation or less than that. Or maybe bread is in a different category that no one ever mentioned to me. Out of nowhere I'm afraid there are rules I don't know about, and I'm worried that nothing I do is going to work.

I breathe in and look around my closet again for an outfit I like—my extra-stretchy jeans and navy top. I get dressed, and I feel okay. The fabric isn't too fitted or itchy. I try harder than I should to look pretty with lip gloss and mascara. But I don't use anything bright or sparkly, because I definitely don't want Benny to know I care as much as I do.

I stay upstairs in my room and avoid eating breakfast until it's time to leave.

Just before 1:00 p.m., Dad drives me to Benny's house. We're a few minutes late, which is way better than showing up early and making things weird.

Dad waits for Benny's mom to answer the door and let me in before he backs out of the driveway and leaves.

"Sarah," Mrs. Saraf says with a smile and a hug, like we're family, instead of people who have never met each other before now. "I'm glad you're here. Benny will be downstairs in a few minutes." The shower is running, and I wonder if he forgot I was coming over or if he just lost track of time.

Benny's mom leads me through the living room and into the kitchen. Everything is new and shiny and stainless steel. There are fancy pots hanging from a rack on the ceiling and a big mixer on the counter. I feel like I walked into a cooking magazine.

There's an old family picture on the wall. The four of them are looking at the camera and smiling. Benny and Asha are holding hands. The only thing I know about Asha, other than that she used to be into music, is that she's a sophomore and the best cross-country runner basically ever. She broke all the school records as a freshman.

"You must be hungry," Benny's mom says. "What can I get you?"

"Oh. I'm okay," I say. "Could I please just have a glass of water?"

"That's it?" Mrs. Saraf sounds disappointed.

"For now," I say, trying to fix whatever I did to mess things up.

"Okay, okay," she says, like she's waving my words away. "I'll just put out a little khoraki in case you change your mind."

Benny's mom pulls containers from the fridge and a tray out of the drawer. She opens a big white cabinet, and from where I'm sitting, I can see that the shelves are stocked with rows of bags and jars and boxes, like at the grocery store. She arranges a huge platter of food and puts the tray in front of me.

"Thank you so much," I say, looking for something safe and approved. Peppers. Carrots. Hummus.

"Eat." She points to the food.

"Mom." Benny's voice is soft but firm.

I turn around, and my heart feels like it's going to explode. His dark brown hair is still wet and combed-through, and he looks cuter than ever. But I don't smile at him or do anything flirty, because he's maybe going to be Emilia's boyfriend, and she's my best friend, so no. Just no. I don't even know why I'm here. I guess because I said I would be, and I didn't want to not show up or cancel and make it seem like I have something to hide, even though I do. And I didn't want to give up my chance to be alone with Benny.

"Benny." Mrs. Saraf nudges him.

"She doesn't have to eat," he says.

"Fine."

"Thank you," I say to his mom.

She walks out of the kitchen without looking back, and I'm not sure what just happened.

Benny sits on the stool next to me. "I'm sorry she tried to force-feed you."

"It's okay."

"Not really. But that's how she is, so, whatever." I'm not sure why Benny says it like he thinks how his mom acts is bad, but before I can ask, he says, "Let's cook something." He starts setting up two stations with cutting boards and knives, and pulls ingredients out from all corners of the kitchen, like he's a magician. *Poof. Pow.* "How do you feel about making garlic-butter salmon with sautéed green beans and roasted potatoes?"

"Oh. Sure. My mom *never* uses butter." The words are out before I realize what I'm saying.

"Why not?" He looks at me like I farted and now the room smells terrible and I ruined this.

"She's really into being healthy."

"But butter isn't bad for you," he says. I want to believe him. But I don't know why he'd be right and Mom would be wrong. "It must be hard to have a mom with rules about eating."

I shrug. "I guess." Because I'm not sure. I don't know any different.

Benny preheats the oven, and then hands me a head of garlic. He shows me how to remove the skin, break up the cloves, peel, and mince. I keep one hand on top of the blade and practice rocking back and forth as I move my knife across the pile until the pieces are fine and even, because apparently consistency is important for flavor. My hand is strained from gripping the knife. I put it down, shake out my wrists, and then try cutting again until the rocking motion starts to feel like it could get easier with practice. Maybe mincing is the dribbling of cooking.

After we're done, Benny shows me how to dice the potatoes, which isn't as hard as mincing garlic, in my opinion, but there are a lot of potatoes.

I've only diced a few when Benny asks, "Have you ever seen Chef Junior?"

"Yeah. I was really into the show for a while."

"Okay. Good. Just checking. Why did you stop watching?"

"It kind of made me sad to think about all the interesting foods that I was missing out on since, you know, everything my parents make basically tastes the same."

"That stinks." He pauses. "I kind of stopped being as into Chef Junior when food got weird here too."

I look up at him, but he's not looking back at me. "Weird how?" I ask.

"My sister is in a treatment place because she won't eat."

My jaw clenches. "I'm sorry," I manage to say.

He puts his pile of potatoes into the bowl between us, and wipes off his knife. "No one knows about Asha," he murmurs, and then goes back to dicing. "It's not her first time. But when she went before, I was sort of glad she was getting help and I wasn't going to have to worry about her anymore. It was going to be someone's actual job to do that. That probably sounds bad. But now I'm scared she's never going to get better, and she's just going to keep disappearing, until she's gone. I get that she wants to be skinny and good at running. But this is like a whole other level." Benny puts the rest of his potatoes and mine into the bowl and covers them with olive oil, salt and pepper, and garlic.

I keep waiting for him to stop moving and cooking, but he tosses the potatoes until they're coated, and then greases two big pans. He spreads them out into one layer, like he wants to give each piece space to breathe.

I stand next to him and take a handful of potatoes. "Is she anorexic?"

"We're not supposed to say that."

I put the potatoes onto the second baking sheet and one slips and falls onto the floor. Neither of us reaches down to pick it up. "She has anorexia. She's sick. She's not the disease."

"Oh," I say. "Sorry."

"It's fine."

We both wash our hands.

He opens the oven, slides the pans inside, and sets the timer. "It's kind of taken over everything. She used to be funny. And she cared about things besides her weight. But she's been sick for so long. It's starting to feel like she's never coming back."

"That sounds really hard." There are so many questions swirling around in my brain, like how and when and why, but I don't need to know the answers or worry, because I'm not going to get an eating disorder. I'm just being healthy.

Benny's eyes are glassy. "It's my fault." He says it like it's a fact. "I got her this runner's app for her birthday so she could track everything, you know—distance, pace, heart rate. I guess it had a calorie counter. The doctor from the first treatment place said there isn't one reason she got sick.

But it's obvious. That's when she started being super strict and obsessed with being healthy. Then she cut out carbs because of something on the app. It just kept getting more intense."

I put my hand on his shoulder. This isn't flirting. This is being nice. He's upset about his sister. "It's not your fault."

"I haven't even told Duke."

"I won't tell," I say. "I really hope she gets better soon."

"Thanks," he says. "I wish it never happened."

"I know what you mean." I wish a lot of things could be completely different.

After Benny flips the potatoes, he shows me how to sauté the green beans and cook the salmon in the pan. The whole kitchen smells like garlic and lemon and butter sizzling together into something warm and comforting.

I flip the fish, and when it's done, Benny plates two meals. And I realize that somehow I completely lost track of time. I haven't looked at my phone or thought about my stomach or Emilia or basketball or anything else since we started cooking. I was focused on following the directions and listening to Benny.

He hands me a fork and waits for me to try mine first.

I drink my water and then refill my glass in the sink,

because I don't know if I can eat what we made. There's butter all over it. And I'm not sure about the potatoes either. They're on Coach Lemon's list. They're just not on Mom's. But butter is not on anyone's list. Only after what Benny told me about his sister, I'm pretty sure I can't tell him about the different lists and why they matter so much. I have to eat in front of Benny—to be a good friend.

It's fine. I didn't eat breakfast, and I can make up for this meal later by eating less at dinner. I don't need to be afraid. I'm not. I'm just being healthy. I pick up my fork and put it into the salmon. The fish is crispy on the outside and soft on the inside. I take a bite, and—"Wow," I say, because it tastes rich and buttery and amazing! It's a million times better than when Mom makes it in the oven.

Benny takes a few big bites, and then smiles at me, lighting up inside. "We crushed this meal."

"Yeah, we did." I smile back.

I eat half the salmon and green beans and one small piece of potato, and then another, because it tastes good and I feel like for right now everything is okay.

On the ride home, the sky is sad and gray and starting to get dark.

I hold on to the container of leftovers Benny packed for me to take home.

Mom taps her French manicured fingernails on the steering wheel. Her hair is pulled back off her face, and she's wearing her fancy purple coat with the big wool flower, because it's Saturday night. Mom and Dad usually go out for dinner. It used to be pizza and movie and babysitter night for me, but that stopped. I'm not sure when. I guess around the time I was old enough to stay home alone. I can't remember if Mom ever checked to make sure I ate enough when I was younger. Maybe that's the kind of thing you don't remember, because it happens all the time. Your brain erases the memory and records something else in its place, because there's not enough space to hold all the regular, not-so-important details. She never worries now. She never even asks.

I turn the knob to change the music. I hate the Coffeehouse station. It reminds me of the dentist.

My phone buzzes in my hand.

That was fun. It's Benny. **Want to cook tomorrow?**

Yes, I text back, because right now that's all I want to do.

Cool. ☺

I type ☺, and then I delete it, because I'm pretty sure sending a smiley face to a boy is flirty.

When Mom stops the car at a red light, she turns to me and says, "Benny is cute."

"He's Emilia's boyfriend." I don't know why I say it. I guess because I need to remind myself that it's going to happen. Benny is off-limits now and always. He has to be. Emilia and Ryan and the team are more important.

"Oh. Okay," Mom says, but she looks confused. "How did it go today? Did you finish your project?"

"It's not really a project. Benny is teaching me how to cook for Chef Junior. It's a YouTube cooking competition. They're filming at school in a few weeks. We get extra credit for health if we participate."

"Hmm," Mom says. "Interesting."

"I need you to sign a form that says I can be on YouTube if we get picked for the show."

"Sure. No problem. I'll sign it tomorrow."

"Thanks," I say. "We made salmon with green beans and potatoes. It was actually really awesome and the food was so good. I did a lot of the cooking! I was thinking that I could help you make dinner on the nights I don't have basketball practice. And maybe our meals could be more like what I made today, you know, with three things."

"What do you mean?" Mom's eyebrows scrunch together. "Three things?"

"I don't know. I guess it just feels nice or complete or something to have more than two foods in a meal." It's weird that I still want Mom to get me more food, even though I'm trying to eat less.

"We have three things a lot," Mom says. "Last week, we had cod, spinach, and salad. And I don't want to say no to you helping with dinner, but I'm not sure it makes sense on school nights when you have homework."

"I can do both," I say quickly.

"Let me think about it."

"Okay," I say, even though that probably means no.

"I can make three things every night if that's what you'd like, but I'd rather not make a carbohydrate with dinner. Potatoes are very starchy."

"Okay," I say softly, because Mom isn't backing down, and I don't want her to ruin this even more than she already has.

"Benny and I are going to practice again tomorrow," I say.

"Great. I can drive you over whenever."

I keep waiting for Mom to ask more questions about the show or about what we're going to cook, but she doesn't. And I don't offer.

Mom wants us to be close and I want that too. I used to talk to her about my actual feelings. I don't know when I stopped. It didn't just happen one day. It wasn't like turning off a faucet. I barely even noticed at first. We started to have less to say to each other. It got quiet and empty and hard to think of words to fill the space unless we were talking about books or basketball. And the music on the radio started to matter more.

Mom parks in the garage, and I follow her into the kitchen. There's an open bag of M&M's on the counter. She rushes to put them away, in the freezer, as fast as she can, and then closes the door with a thud. She walks out of the room without looking at me, like the candy is her secret. She's ashamed. I am too.

I put my food in the fridge and go upstairs to my room to read my book.

An hour later, Dad knocks. "We're leaving for dinner in a few minutes. I picked up a falafel sandwich and baklava from Rami's on my way home from basketball."

"Thanks," I say, and for a second, it doesn't matter that I can't eat those foods, because Dad wants to make sure I have the things I need. "Did you win?" I ask.

"You know it." He smiles. "Mom and I shouldn't be out

too late. But call if you need anything. It's one of those places Mom hates, with a lot of courses, so I'm sure she'd be happy to cut out early." He says it like he thinks it's quirky and cute. And I wonder if I'm making too big a deal out of Mom's eating, since Dad knows how she is and doesn't seem worried, or if hiding problems in plain sight is another thing that's easy for Mom, like being pretty.

He hugs me and kisses my forehead. "Make sure you have a little fun tonight, okay? Watch a movie or something."

I nod. "I will."

I don't eat the dinner Dad bought me. I finish the salmon and green beans I made with Benny, and stay up way too late texting Emilia and Ryan and watching clips from Chef Junior on YouTube.

In the morning, my stomach is hollow, and my clothes don't feel as tight as they did yesterday, because I ate less and no bread. It feels like I finally know all the rules.

At Benny's house, we make his family chicken recipe with turmeric and lime, cucumber salad, and rice. I don't think about how I'm eventually going to have to eat this meal, because I'd rather be in the moment and cook. And even though the recipe is totally different, I'm a little more comfortable dicing and mincing and moving around the kitchen today than I was yesterday.

I can follow along with the recipe, and I know where to be and what needs to happen next, even if I don't know how to do all the different things.

Benny walks me through each step. He even shows me some of his mom's tricks, like using crushed garlic, fresh squeezed lime juice, and plenty of sea salt, to add extra flavor.

When the food is ready, he explains how to plate the entrées, like we're at a fancy restaurant, and then he lets me try. I scoop the rice with a measuring cup, and place the chicken on top to make a pyramid. On the other side of the plate, I arrange the cucumber salad. Not to brag, but the meal looks super profesh!

I try a few bites of chicken and cucumber salad. They're both so good. And it feels like Benny and I could maybe be a real team.

I'm about to take a bite of rice, because I'm eating in front of Benny, when Mom rings the doorbell. So I pack up my plate and leave without having to break my rules.

SEVEN

THE WEEK OF THE DANCE goes by quickly. I keep getting better and faster in basketball. Pretty soon it will be like the first part of the season never even happened.

Every time I see Emilia in the courtyard, in the hall between classes, at lunch, even during practice, I think about telling her that I was at Benny's house this weekend learning how to cook, because we're competing together in Chef Junior. Only I can't. I don't want things to be awkward between us. Emilia is my BFF. I'd pick her over Benny. The fact that I'm partners with him shouldn't matter. But I know it still does.

On Friday after school, Ryan's mom picks all three of us

up, because Emilia and I are both getting ready at Ryan's house and sleeping over after the dance.

There are potato chips and chicken nuggets on the coffee table in the family room. It doesn't matter that I'm hungry or that the air smells salty and fried. None of the food on that table is an option for me, because we're having pizza after the dance. I thought about pretending I couldn't sleep over, but I didn't want to have to deal with Mom. That seemed worse.

I fill up my water bottle, drink as much as I can, and try not to breathe in or look at the plate of nuggets with multiple dipping sauces that's so close I could just reach out and grab a handful.

Emilia snacks while she curls my hair, spraying and smoothing and clipping until I have perfect waves. She does my makeup too, and when she's finished, she says, "Voilà!" and hands me a mirror.

I look pretty. My eyes are lined with plum and my pink cheeks pop.

She grabs another handful of chips and sits down in the chair next to me. "Why aren't you eating anything?"

"I'm not hungry," I say.

"But you missed lunch."

My stomach dips. "No, I didn't," I say back. "I just ate in the library. I had to finish my French homework. I'm always behind lately."

Emilia eats another nugget and sighs. "Okay, so, don't be mad at me for telling you this, but a few girls on the team think something's wrong, like maybe you're on a diet. They're really worried about you."

"What? Who?"

Emilia shakes her head. "It doesn't matter."

"It does to me."

"Fine." She folds her arms. "Tamar and Sage."

They don't care about me. But I don't say that. Emilia thinks they do. "I'm not on a diet," I say. "But, like, why would that be a big deal anyway?"

"Um, because diets are the worst. They're so bad for you. Not everyone knows that. But it's true. My doctor told me. And she's not just a regular doctor. She's, like, an expert on being healthy."

"Weird," Ryan says. "I feel like so many adults go on them."

Emilia rolls her eyes. "That's because they're obsessed with being skinny. They think it means you're better at life, which is stupid and rude to everyone who isn't. Also, Lizzo is way better at singing and dancing and performing and being confident and pretty than basically everyone, and she's not small."

"Yeah," I say. "Totes."

Ryan is nodding.

"I'll tell them you're not on a diet," Emilia says. "But they were maybe going to tell Coach Lemon that you aren't eating."

What? No. They can't do that. "Are you serious?"

"I told them not to. But I don't know what they're going to do."

"They're obviously jealous," Ryan says. "I bet they thought they had a chance to start in basketball. But you proved them wrong."

"Maybe." Emilia shrugs. "I mean, you have lost weight. That's like a fact. It's kind of obvious. And Coach Lemon said we should watch out for one another. We're teammates."

"It actually can't be a fact, because (A) I don't weigh myself and (B) I don't even have a scale." Right now that feels like proof that I'm totally fine.

"Okay," Emilia says, backing down. "I just thought you should know, because we're BFFs, and I wouldn't want people talking about me like that behind my back."

116

"Thanks for telling me," I say, because it's not Emilia's fault. I just don't need Tamar and Sage keeping track of what I eat. I'm doing enough of that on my own. But I can't say what I'm really thinking out loud, and I need to show Emilia that she should be on my side, so I pick up a chicken nugget, dip it in ketchup, and pop it into my mouth, like it's not a big deal. It's crunchy and salty and wrong. Even after I swallow, I can still taste the crispy breading. Then my stomach growls, reminding me I'm hungry. I hope Ryan and Emilia didn't hear that, because I can't eat anymore. Nuggets aren't on the lists.

"Don't worry," Ryan says. "We'll back you up. And Coach Lemon will definitely believe us over them. She knows how much they love drama."

"Okay," I say. "Thanks." I take a deep breath and try to calm down. I wish I could tell Ryan and Emilia the truth—that I'm hungry and tired of counting and worrying, but I don't know how to stop.

We're thirty minutes late to the dance because Emilia decided at the last minute we needed to paint our nails. Mine are already smudged, and I have to be careful, because they're still sticky. I wanted to say no to the impromptu manicure, but after everything else, I didn't think I should.

When we finally walk into the dance, a song I don't

immediately recognize is playing. It's new and electronic, but the words are familiar. If I tried hard enough, I might be able to find the lyrics somewhere in the way back of my brain.

Benny is in the middle of the room with Duke. He's smiling and bopping his head to the beat. My stomach flutters. I turn away before someone notices me.

Tamar and Sage are standing by the door waiting for us, like they're part of our group. It bothers me more now that I know they've been talking behind my back. I wish Emilia would hurry up and figure out that they're not actually that nice, so what they think of me and what I eat for lunch won't matter.

"Fashionable." Sage nods.

Emilia shrugs. "We lost track of time."

"We should all get ready together before the next dance," Tamar says.

"Done." Emilia answers for us.

The song changes to something fast and fun. I keep waiting for everyone in our circle to rush over to the dance floor. But no one moves.

"I didn't know you signed up for Chef Junior," Tamar says to me.

I bite down, trying to hide my fear.

"You did?" Emilia looks confused. "You didn't tell us that."

Tamar twirls one of her long ringlets. "But she told you that she's tight with Benny, right?"

"I'm not," I say back.

"But you're partners . . . for Chef Junior."

My chest tightens. I need to breathe and think fast and find a way to explain.

"What are you talking about?" Emilia asks Tamar, and then looks at me.

"It's extra credit for class," I say.

"Mm-hmm," Sage says. "We all definitely believe you."

"The partners were assigned." My voice catches in my throat.

"The *health* partners were assigned," Emilia says. "You didn't have to enter Chef Junior with him."

"Or practice at his house all weekend," Tamar adds.

Emilia's eyebrows jump to the top of her forehead. "Seriously?"

"Just admit it." Sage glares at me. "You love Benny."

"Do you?" Emilia asks, like it hadn't occurred to her until right now that Benny and me were even possible, like she's realizing for the first time that I'm the competition.

I shake my head. "I don't." My voice is firm and confident. I feel horrible for lying to her. But I can't like him. It's not allowed. I need to just stop having a crush on him. "I don't know how to cook, and he's teaching me so I'm ready for the audition."

"Okay." She drags out the word. "But it's kind of weird that you didn't tell me."

"We're just friends," I say. "It's not what you think. I wanted to tell you." It feels good to say something true. Even if it's not the whole truth.

"So . . ." Sage says. "Why didn't you?"

Everyone is staring at me waiting for my answer. I just need to explain that I wasn't sure how to tell her, but before I can, Emilia says, "I actually don't care. It doesn't matter. It's fine. And not to be rude, but I'd much rather dance than stand around dealing with this dumb drama."

"Ditto," Ryan says.

Emilia grabs on to Ryan and Ryan grabs on to me and we walk toward the music and over to where Benny and Duke are dancing.

I should feel relieved that Emilia doesn't care. We're still BFFs. But I feel sick to my stomach and more afraid than before, because now she knows I could like Benny. Everyone does. It was hard enough to hide how I felt when Emilia wasn't watching.

I try not to look at Benny and Emilia. I keep my eyes on Ryan and the floor and the crowd. I'm mad at him for telling people about Chef Junior when he said he wouldn't, when he promised he would keep my secret.

After a few fast songs, the music slows down.

Duke asks Ryan to dance.

Everyone starts to pair off. Tamar is dancing with an eighth-grade boy and Sage is arm in arm with someone from the basketball team. I don't want to stand here by myself, so I turn and walk out. That's when I see Emilia and Benny swaying together with barely any space between them, like they could maybe be a real couple.

My heart hurts.

I walk down the hall to a bathroom that's close enough so I can still hear the music, but far enough away that no one will find me. I hide in the last stall, open a book I downloaded on my phone, and read until the dance is over.

Just after the DJ announces the last song, Ryan ducks under the door, and says, "Open up."

I unlock the latch and let her in.

She sits down on the floor next to me. "I didn't think

you liked him anymore." Her voice is so soft I almost miss it.

"I don't know how to stop," I whisper. "I keep trying, but I can't."

Ryan puts her arm around me. "That sounds kind of impossible."

"Yeah," I say, leaning into her. It doesn't matter that Ryan has never had a crush on anyone before, because she gets that this hurts and it's nice not to be the only one who knows how sad I am. "I should have just told Emilia I liked him at the beginning of the year. But I wanted her to like me, and I didn't know how to say it. And then the same thing happened with Chef Junior."

Ryan squeezes my shoulder.

"What do you think I should do?" I ask.

"I mean, you should be honest. But I get why you weren't. She makes it kind of hard. It's like she doesn't want anyone to actually tell her the truth."

It feels good that Ryan gets why I didn't tell Emilia, even if I should have. I sigh. "Tonight is going to be so awkward."

She shakes her head. "It'll be okay. Promise."

At Ryan's house, there's a stack of pizzas on the counter.

Ryan finishes two slices while we're getting plates and drinks.

Her mom didn't order salads or anything other than pizza and cheesy breadsticks, which means there's nothing else to fill my plate, so I hide out in the bathroom and stall, because I can only have one slice.

When I finally sit down at the table and start eating, my hunger hits me all at once. And before I realize what's happening, I'm done with my piece. It's gone, even the crust. Mrs. Martin slides another slice onto my plate, clears the empty box away, and puts a fresh pizza in the middle of the table.

I drink all my water and then refill my glass.

"Thirsty?" Emilia shoots me an I See Right Through You look.

"Yeah," I say. "I'm so dehydrated."

I keep waiting for her to turn away, but she doesn't. I don't get why she cares what I eat or don't eat. She got everything she wanted. Benny picked her. They danced. Everyone saw them. It's basically official now. They're going to be boyfriend-girlfriend. I wish she'd leave me alone about this one thing that's mine.

I pick up my second slice and take a small bite. Only once I start eating, I can't stop. And as soon as I'm done, I wish I could press rewind. I can't lose basketball. It's the only thing

I have left. I don't care that there's going to be dessert later. I need to stop eating and be perfect tomorrow. I can eat less than I normally do, because I'll be home, without my friends.

"Are you girls okay?" Mrs. Martin asks. "Everyone's so quiet."

"We're tired," Ryan says quickly.

"Okay, well, don't stay up too late. We have our meeting tomorrow. It's an important day for our family." Mrs. Martin gives Ryan a look I've never seen before, like she better be ready, because whatever they're doing matters a lot.

"Got it." Ryan's words are sharp.

"I'm heading to bed. There's another pizza in the fridge and leftover burgers and there are plenty of snacks downstairs. Oh, and I made chocolate chip cookies." It's strange how the endless options used to make me feel safe, but right now, I wish Ryan's mom would quit talking about food, because my stomach is big and bloated inside my jeans, and all I want to do is go to bed so I can stop thinking about how bad I feel.

"Yeah. Okay. We know. Thanks, Mom."

"Good night." Mrs. Martin walks out of the kitchen and up the stairs. I'm about to ask Ryan if she's okay, but she's already shaking her head, like she doesn't want to talk or think about tomorrow.

124

We're all quiet for a minute.

I look at Emilia. "I'm sorry I didn't tell you that I like Benny. I've been trying really hard not to, because I don't want to fight over a boy. And I get that it seems weird that I went to his house to cook and didn't say anything to you about it, but I swear—"

"I don't care that you have a crush on Benny," Emilia interrupts. "You don't have to tell people who you like. That's your private business. But not telling me about Chef Junior, that's weak."

I chew my lip. "I know," I say. "I'm sorry."

"It doesn't even matter now. Tamar said he's definitely asking me out, probably tomorrow."

"That's great!" I try really hard to sound happy for her, because I am, even though I'm sad for me.

Emilia smiles. "Thanks. We're totally meant to be." Then she turns to Ryan. "What's up with you and Duke?"

"Nothing." Ryan opens the pizza box and takes another slice.

"Don't lie," Emilia says. "You danced together twice."

"You did?" I ask.

Ryan is looking down at her plate.

"OMG! You love him," Emilia says.

"I don't," Ryan snaps. "We've said like four words to each other. And Tamar would hate me."

Emilia smirks. "Oh. I'm pretty sure she already does."

"Great. That's just perfect. That's exactly what the team needs. More fighting over stupid boys." Ryan isn't talking about boys from school anymore. She's talking about her brothers and how their basketball always matters more than everything else.

"The team always comes first," I say to Ryan. "Cross my heart."

Ryan nods, and then looks at Emilia.

But Emilia is looking down, smiling at something on her phone. It feels like she's not here anymore, and like it's my fault she's gone.

EIGHT

THERE ARE BLUEBERRY muffins for breakfast. Emilia asks if I want to split one, and I say yes without thinking. She's acting like nothing has changed and like Chef Junior really doesn't matter to her. And maybe it actually doesn't matter, because I'm too mad at Benny to keep cooking with him anyway. Only I can't eat half or part or even one bite of a muffin. Mom has a lot of opinions about muffins, so I know they're not on her list. I'm scared that if I mess up two days in a row, I'll never get back to my plan.

I drink a glass of water to avoid eating.

My stomach grumbles. I'm hungry, which makes no

sense. I went to bed full of pizza. It feels like that never happened, even though it definitely did. It turns out eating makes me hungry.

Emilia is already finished with her half. She's staring at my plate. It's a competition. Or it's a test that I can't pass without breaking my own rules. Either way, I'm trapped. I don't want to be here anymore. I want to go back to before I ate the wrong things and ruined everything.

The doorbell rings. A minute later, I hear Dad talking to Mrs. Martin in the front hall. I say bye to my friends and wrap my muffin in a napkin, like I'm going to eat it in the car or when I get home.

Only I don't. I throw it away in our kitchen trash. Then I change and meet Dad outside to shoot hoops.

We both do a few "around the world" shooting drills. I usually love playing basketball with Dad. He's always encouraging, but today it isn't helping me feel better. Everything is still bad, even this.

It's like the food from last night is making me feel like my body has changed all over again, even though I sort of know that's impossible and that's just how it feels in my head. But I can't think about anything else.

When I finally get back up to my room, my phone

is humming on my bed. It's Benny: **Want to practice tomorrow? T-minus two weeks until auditions.**

I want to tell him we're not partners anymore because I'm so mad at him for telling people about Chef Junior when he said he wouldn't and I'm mad at myself for trusting him and maybe a little for liking him when I shouldn't have. Only I don't write back. I ignore him for now, because I don't want to quit and not compete. I like cooking.

I need to talk to Emilia. It doesn't matter that things are still weird and that texting her about Benny is not going to help. She's my best friend, and he's going to be her boyfriend or he already is. I don't want to mess up again and make things even worse.

Hey. What's up? I text Emilia, and immediately regret pressing send, because my message is awkward. I stare at my words, waiting for her to answer. But she doesn't. Not right away. I flip my phone over. She said she wasn't mad. We danced and ate pizza and she asked me to split a muffin, and even though I didn't actually eat it, we're not in a fight. Everything is fine.

My phone buzzes in my hand. It's Emilia! *Phew.* **Not much. Hanging out.**

Cool. I need to just tell her the truth. **Benny asked if we**

could practice tomorrow for Chef Junior. Is that okay?

Your call. There's a lump in my throat. I'm about to ask what she means, but then my phone buzzes again. **GTG.**

Wait, I text. **Can we talk?**

No. Bye.

The lump swells. I clear my throat and cough, but nothing helps. I can barely breathe. It doesn't matter that Emilia said we were fine. We're not. She's mad at me, and I'm not sure how to make it better, so I do the only thing I can think of: I call Ryan. "Can you talk?" I ask as soon as she picks up.

"Yeah. Of course," she says, but she sounds sad.

"How's it going?" I want to tell her everything that just happened with Emilia but I know meeting with college scouts isn't fun for her and I want to make sure she's okay before I start talking about me.

"I don't know . . . Bad." She sighs, like she's too tired to explain. "It hasn't been announced yet, but they committed to UNC, so everything is about to get way worse. It's going to be all about their basketball for the rest of my life. And I get that I should be happy, because this is good for me too. My parents can't pay for all of us to go to college. But I don't know. It just makes me not want to play anymore. There's like no point. Even if I get to the WNBA,

I can't make a living playing basketball. It's not fair."

"Ry—"

"I know."

Ryan talks about quitting basketball a lot, basically whenever she's feeling extra invisible to her family, which really stinks. I know she's not going to stop playing. Even when it feels like we'll never count as much in sports because we're girls. "Small wins," I say, because I want her to know she can keep going and trying and proving she matters and we matter, even if she shouldn't have to.

"Small wins," she says.

We're both quiet for a minute, and then she asks, "What's up with you?"

"Nothing," I say. "It's not important."

"It is. Tell me."

I take a breath. "Emilia is so mad at me. I might drop out of Chef Junior."

"No. Don't. Unless you don't want to compete anymore. Benny shouldn't get in the way of what you want."

"I know, but I really messed up. Emilia is acting like she hates me. And I need to find a way to fix it."

"You can't." My heart stops. "You said sorry and explained your side, so there's like basically nothing else you can do.

131

She'll get over it eventually. Quitting now isn't going to change anything with Emilia."

"Really?" I wish Ryan would tell me what Emilia said after I left her house, because I'm pretty sure they had a whole talk about me and Benny, and now there are things I don't know that Ryan isn't telling me.

"I'm one hundred percent sure. And don't keep bringing it up. That's only going to make it worse."

"But I already did."

"It'll be okay," she says. "Even if it's not. Ugh. I have to go. My mom is waving me over. Sorry."

"It's fine."

"Bye," she says, and hangs up.

It's Saturday night. Mom and Dad are going out. Dad went to Provini and bought a bunch of different dishes. And Mom left the cozy blankets for me by the TV, a list of movies we've been talking about watching, and two new library books with a sticky note: **I accidentally read seventy-five pages of this one. ☺ Love, Mom**

I wrap myself in fleece, snuggle up on the sofa, and start *High-Rise*. It's so good. I end up reading for a while, until I can't concentrate anymore because I'm too hungry. I try to think about how much better I'll feel tomorrow and how much faster I'll be in the game on Monday if I don't eat before bed. But my stomach hurts, and I can't stop myself from going into the kitchen and shoveling a bunch of carrots and an apple with almond butter into my mouth.

Our kitchen is careless and temporary, like we're about to move or we just did. Even though we never have. There are crumbs in the silverware drawer that have been there forever. It looks like the small bits of granola that collect at the bottom of the bag. Only Mom doesn't buy granola.

I take the salad from Provini and the leftovers from Mom and Dad's dinner last night—salmon and asparagus—out of the fridge, and the aluminum foil that covers the pan falls onto the floor. The edges weren't even folded over. I take a fork and knife, and eat the cold, mushy vegetables, salmon, and salad. I eat and eat—I know I need to stop but I can't, and when I look down again, all the food is gone.

I put my dish in the sink, run the hot water, and rinse it out. My stomach is pushing against my pants. I want the food to go away. I lift up my shirt and look. I can't help imagining everything I just ate expanding in my stomach. I stick the pan into the dishwasher and shut the door.

133

It doesn't matter that all the food was on both lists. I still feel like I did something wrong.

I get into bed and write back to Benny. **You shouldn't have told Tamar we were partners. You said you wouldn't.**

I didn't, he texts back right away. **I swear. Coach Lemon left the list on her desk, and Tamar looked at the names and told everyone.**

OMG. That's what happened?

Yeah. I'm not a jerk.

I sort of wish he was, because then it would be a lot easier to stop liking him, or maybe I never would have liked him in the first place and I would have told Emilia about Chef Junior, and everything would be different. **I know that. But then how did Tamar find out we cooked at your house?**

She asked me if we were good, so I said she should watch out, because we've been practicing.

K, I write. I can't be mad at him. It's not like I told him the real reason I didn't want anyone to know about Chef Junior. **I'm just not sure I want to compete.**

Please don't quit, he texts. **Chef Junior is going to be so fun. Don't you want to know the four mystery**

ingredients? And figure out how to make them work together? And maybe get on the show? I really think we can win.

I do too. And Emilia said it's my call. I can do what I want. Plus, Ryan said nothing I do is going to change things with Emilia. **Okay. I'll be there.**

Yes!!!

The next day, I wake up early. I try to fall back asleep, but I'm hungry, and no matter what I do, I'm awake. I bring my book downstairs and eat my yogurt as slowly as I can while I read. But then there's nothing left in my bowl, and I'm still so hungry.

A few minutes later, Dad sits down next to me. "Let's go out for breakfast. I'm in the mood for pancakes or waffles. We should get both." He sounds excited, and a big plate of chocolate chip pancakes with Vermont maple syrup would taste so good.

"I just ate," I say.

"Eat again."

"I don't feel that great. I couldn't really sleep."

Dad puts his hand on my forehead, like he's sure my problem is the kind with symptoms and solutions, even though it's not. I don't have a fever or a stomachache.

I put my elbows on the table and rest my head in my hands. "I got into a fight with Emilia. I thought it was over. But she's still mad. There's nothing I can do to make it better. Ryan even said. And I'm pretty sure it's never really going to be okay again." I know it's true as soon as I say it. Even if she does eventually get over the fact that I kept secrets from her, it's the kind of fight that's going to be there from now on, stuck between us, like gum, making everything a little sticky.

"I'm sorry," Dad says.

"It's my fault." I stop myself, because I realize Dad and I have never actually talked about boys or crushes and it might be awkward. But also, I don't care if it is. I want to tell him. "We like the same boy. Only I didn't tell Emilia I had a crush on him, or that we're partners for Chef Junior. And then she found out."

"That's tricky." Dad nods. "But there's nothing wrong with liking the same boy. You can't help who you like."

"I tried really hard to stop."

Dad puts a hand on my shoulder. "Emilia probably just needs time to get over the fact that you didn't tell her about Chef Junior."

"I hope so."

"You look tired, kiddo. You should try to go back to sleep

or at least get into bed and rest. I can take you out for break-fast when you're up again."

"Okay. I'll try," I say, and then walk upstairs, because I'm pretty sure going to my room and staying there is the only way to avoid eating pancakes.

I get back into bed and read until it's almost time to leave for Benny's house. I shower and change into a sweat-shirt that's big enough so I can hide a little, but not so baggy that it looks like it swallowed me. I'm finishing my hair when my phone buzzes. It's a text from Ryan: **Pickup game downtown in an hour. Emilia will be there. Come.**

Are you sure? There's no way she wants me there.

She needs to get over it. We have a game tomorrow. And I want to win.

I'm about to tell Ryan that I can't because I'm cooking with Benny, but I stop myself. I want to play basketball and make things better with Emilia. And after the weekend Ryan had, I don't think it's a great idea to say I can't come because of a boy, even if I really do want to cook. **Me too! Text me when you get there.**

Obvs! ☺

Then I text Benny: **I can't cook today. I have to do something for the team. Sorry.**

What about after?

I want to say yes, but it doesn't seem like a great idea to make plans today in case the pickup game is fun and everyone hangs out after. I don't want to have to explain that I'm leaving early to cook with Benny. **Not sure when it's going to end.**

Roger. Maybe this week?

I don't have practice on Wednesday.

That works, he texts. **Bummed about today.**

I want to write *me too*, but I don't.

On the ride downtown, fear flips around in my stomach, making me carsick. I think about telling Dad I might puke. I know he'll turn around and take me home without asking questions. Ryan would believe me too. But I told her I'd be there, and I'm not backing out on her now.

Usually I'm fine to show up early for practice or plans with my friends, but this doesn't feel like a regular hangout, so I make Dad park across the street and wait until Ryan texts me that she's here.

"Are you sure you're all right?" Dad asks.

"Yeah." I force a smile. "Just nervous."

"Okay. Call me if you need anything. I can be here in a few minutes."

"I will," I say. "Thanks."

Inside, it smells like fruit punch and graham crackers. When I get to the gym, Ryan is standing on the court by herself, eating a Clif Bar and drinking orange juice. "Want some?" She holds the bottle out to me.

"I'm okay," I say, because juice is all empty calories. I'm not sure what those are exactly, but I know Mom thinks they're really bad. Only as soon as I turn Ryan down, I think about all the food she's seen me not eat recently. And I'm worried she's going to notice. "My dad took me for pancakes earlier." The words are out before I can stop myself from lying to Ryan.

"Really? Where?"

"The diner," I say.

"Wait, so weird. What time? We were there too—to celebrate my brothers, obvi."

"No way!" But then I don't know what to say, and I need to think of something fast, because we're just standing here in silence, waiting for me to answer her question. That's when I remember her brothers always sleep in late. "Early. I couldn't sleep, because of the fight."

"Sorry." Her face falls. Then she opens her mouth like maybe she's about to say something else, but before she can,

Tamar walks in with Emilia and Sage flanked on either side of her. I wonder if they all came from one of their houses or if they just showed up at the same time and walked in as a group.

A few other girls from the team follow behind them. Emilia doesn't look at me. She looks everywhere else. Then she whispers something to Sage, and Sage says something back, and they both laugh. I swallow and try to ignore my stomach twisting into knots. I don't get what happened between the last time we talked and now. I mean, I get that she's mad, but she texted me back, and now she won't even make eye contact with me.

There aren't enough of us to play five-on-five, but the gym is smaller than regulation size, so we can play full-court. And since it's pickup, we get to improvise, which is way more fun for me.

Once we're running and passing, I manage to push everything else out of my head and get lost in the game. I make bucket after bucket.

We don't switch teams. We just play one long game. No one says it's because things are too awkward with Emilia and me, but it's obvious.

I do my part on offense and defense—moving together

with my teammates in rhythm with one goal: to win.

And we do!

When we're done, I'm tired and a little light-headed from running hard. I sit on the floor by my bag while we all grab water. A few girls pass around snacks, but it's nothing I can actually eat. I act like I'm interested in the popcorn, but I don't take any, and then I get up and hand the bag to Emilia, because she's next to me.

"I saw what you did." Her eyes narrow. "Just admit you're trying to be skinny because you're obsessed with Benny."

"What? No," I say. Being healthy has nothing to do with Benny. But I can't say any of that out loud.

"You're such a liar." She shoots me a look, like I'm smelly old leftovers. "No offense, but boys don't like girls who don't eat. They think it's weird."

"I eat," I say.

"Lettuce doesn't count."

"Can we please talk about basketball or the team?" Ryan cuts in.

"Well, she's not going to be on the team for much longer," Sage says. "Coach Lemon hates diets and when she finds out—"

"Give it up," Ryan shouts. "Sarah is not on a diet!"

Emilia snorts. "Whatever." She rolls her eyes at Ryan and then looks at me. "You're going to blow up once you start eating like a normal person again. And you will eventually. No one can be all perfect and in control forever. And diets mess with your body and make you gain back more weight. That's how it works. It's, like, science. Sorry. But it's going to happen. And when it does, we'll all know you were lying, so good luck with that."

That can't be true. I mean, no. Emilia has to be wrong. Why would anyone ever diet if that were real? But I don't say anything. I'm afraid if I open my mouth, everything I'm feeling will come pouring out of me, and then Emilia will know she's right that I've been eating less.

"What's your problem?" Ryan says to Emilia.

"I don't want to be friends with someone who's controlling about food. It stresses me out. Plus, Sarah lied about Chef Junior, and now I kind of don't believe anything she says. So yeah, we're not friends anymore." Emilia's words punch me in the face. Hard. Sharp. Pain. Then she turns around and walks out of the gym. Tamar and Sage and the other girls follow behind her.

Before I realize what's happening, I'm crying.

Ryan hugs me, like she's trying as hard as she can to

make this better. But she can't. I want to turn off the voices and ignore the rules and forget about the lists. I hate them. But it's like they're always there now, getting louder and stronger.

"I'm sorry," she says. "I thought this would be way different."

I nod. "Me too. But I mean, I lied to her, so I get why she's mad."

"Okay, fine, but she didn't even want to talk more or see your side of things. She was just rude." Ryan sighs. And when she breathes out, the air around us is heavy.

"Thanks for having my back," I say.

"Always," Ryan says, then she holds her drink out to me.

I should put the straw between my lips and force myself to take a sip. Just one. Ryan defended me and I need her. But I have to say no. Juice is bad. It's not on Mom's list. It won't be okay.

I shake my head. "I'm good."

I keep waiting for Ryan to insist or ask me questions about what I've been eating, but she doesn't. And I'm not sure if it's because she doesn't actually want to share her juice or if it's because she knows I'm lying to her too.

* * *

"How did you play?" Dad asks as soon as I get in the car.

"Really well." My words get stuck in my throat.

There's '80s music on the radio. It's fun and upbeat, and I know Dad turned it on for me. It makes me wish everything were different.

He squeezes my shoulder. "Buckle up, sweetheart. We'll be home soon."

Neither of us says anything else on the ride, but after Dad parks in the garage and we get out of the car, he walks over and gives me a big bear hug. I hold on to him, and don't let go for a few minutes. I'm wearing a sweatshirt and a coat, so I'm pretty sure he can't tell anything about me has changed that much, and at least for right now, it feels like he can protect me.

"Want to talk about what happened?" he asks.

"Emilia hates me." I want to tell him that she's going to try and get me kicked off the team, but I can't, because I don't want him to ask why. "I ruined everything. I should have just told her about Chef Junior."

Dad rubs my back. "Go easy on yourself, honey. You apologized."

"It's not good enough." My voice is shaky.

"If she really can't see your side of things, she might not be the kind of friend you need."

"That's not how it works, Dad." I back away from him. "She's on my team and she's friends with my friends."

I keep waiting for him to say something that will make this better for me. "I'm sorry, Sar. I really am." And I know he is, but it doesn't help at all.

Our whole house smells like soup. There's a big pot on the stove, and the table is set. Mom also made chicken and a salad with peppers, cucumbers, and tomatoes. Three things. I wonder if it's because of what I said.

"Sit." Mom grins at Dad and at me. "Who wants soup? It's only vegetables and vegetable broth. It's very healthy."

I raise my hand. Dad does too.

"It smells amazing," he says.

"I hope it tastes good. You know I never follow a recipe. I make it up as I go." She puts a bowl down in front of me and Dad, and then gets soup for herself. We wait for Mom to sit before we start eating.

The soup tastes bland, but it feels warm and safe and approved, and I never want it to end. Mom and I finish at the same time, and when I'm done, I get seconds, because I'm hungry. I have plain salad, no dressing, and a piece of chicken about the size of my hand.

After we eat for a little while, Mom asks, "So, what do you think of *High-Rise?*"

"It's amazing!" I say. "I mean, I already started making a chart, so I know I'm really into it."

Her eyebrows pinch. "Chart?"

"It's like a list of clues that matter and also, you know, my working theories for what might have happened."

"Oooh, let me see!" Mom sounds excited.

It makes me excited too. I stand up and get my notebook from my backpack, open to the last page, and hand the chart to Mom.

When she looks down at my notes, her eyes light up. "This is really impressive, Sarah," she says, without looking up from my work.

"Thanks!" I say.

"I came up with your first theory too," Mom says.

"But it's too obvious, right?"

"Exactly. It feels distracting, like that's what the author wants us to think. But your second theory—that's really smart. It has to be right." She looks up at me. "I never would have seen that." Mom is beaming, like she's so proud that I'm hers, like I did something important.

I can't stop smiling. I wish I could soak up this happy feeling and put it in a bottle like a potion to save for the next time she forgets dinner. But I guess I know that's not possible. The good feelings aren't magic. They don't have the power to erase the bad ones.

It doesn't seem like we've been eating for very long when Mom gets up and starts clearing the table. My plate and bowl are both empty. But I don't want dinner to end. I want our family to be like this every night. Mom is already opening the dishwasher.

"Can I have more soup?" I ask, because I want to rewind and go back.

"You're still hungry?" Mom sounds worried or annoyed. I can't tell. Either way, it feels like I did something wrong.

"Actually, never mind," I say.

"Are you sure?" Dad asks. "There's plenty."

"Yeah. I'm sure." I stand up and help Mom and Dad clear the table, because we have a game tomorrow, so even if the soup is healthy, it's better if I don't eat too much.

After I finish my homework, I go back downstairs to fill up my water bottle with ice. I'm about to walk into the kitchen when I hear Mom say, "I don't think we have anything to worry about. She ate chicken and salad and two bowls of soup." I stop walking and hold my breath.

"Liv, that soup is made of nothing," Dad says.

"It's made of vitamins and nutrients," Mom says back.

The kettle whistles, loud and angry.

I turn around and tiptoe as quietly as I can back down the hall toward the stairs and around the corner, where my parents can't see me, but close enough so I can still hear them, just in case they take their tea into the family room.

Someone turns off the stove and pours the boiling water. Based on the footsteps, I'm pretty sure it's Dad. "She looks different," he says. "I guess that shouldn't matter, as long as she's eating enough and taking care of herself."

"It really seems like she is," Mom says.

Dad sighs. "I don't know. She barely ate anything I brought home from Provini the other day."

"Maybe she wasn't in the mood for Italian. Those meals can be hard on your stomach and very heavy. I think she ate plenty tonight. She always eats plenty. She has a healthy appetite."

Something about the way Mom says "healthy appetite" bothers me. I wonder if maybe a food I ate is only good in moderation, and I accidentally ate too much without realizing.

"I'm just worried. Middle school is hard, and she had a tough start to the season, and now she's in a fight with Emilia."

"I didn't know they had a fight." Mom says it like now she's worried too. "Tell me everything."

"All I know is that they like the same boy."

"Oh no," Mom says. "Fighting with your friends is the worst. Maybe I should talk to her?"

"She'll talk to you when she's ready."

"You're right. I don't want to push."

And even though I don't want my parents to worry about me, it feels good to know they care.

NINE

IN THE MORNING, there's no yogurt in the fridge or eggs or anything except leftover soup and condiments. It's like every time Mom remembers a meal, she forgets one. And now I'm mad that I asked if we could have three things for dinner. It was too much. I should have kept my opinions to myself. But I obviously had to make a big deal about how I wanted dinner to be different, and now there's nothing for breakfast.

I close the fridge because it's sad in there and the smell of soup is starting to make me queasy. I'm pretty sure if I shut the door right now, I can forget about the empty shelves and the feeling that I'm not worth feeding or caring about or loving. If I were, there would be food.

On the ride to school, I turn up the music and try to forget I'm hungry. I don't say anything to Mom about the fact that there was nothing to eat. Talking about food just makes everything worse.

There's no one in the courtyard when Mom drops me off. It's too cold to stand outside. I walk toward the entrance and keep my head down. The wind whistles and pushes up against my puffy coat, sending a chill through even the smallest gaps in my layers of clothing.

Inside, it's warm and crowded. I wasn't running or even walking that fast, but I need to stop and catch my breath. I take out my water bottle and gulp down as much as I can, because my throat is dry, and it feels like I haven't had anything to drink today, even though I obviously have.

I hear snickering a few feet away. Tamar and Sage are huddled in the corner. It's not just them. Other kids are staring too. Their eyes are all over me. I'm pretty sure by now everyone knows that Emilia ditched me. But she isn't with her new besties, which means she's probably with Benny being flirty and girlfriend-y. I need to stop thinking about that now, when I already feel sick.

I weave through the maze of kids and coats and

backpacks, searching around the lobby for Ryan, because I can't stand alone in the middle of everyone. Not now. But she isn't here again, so I lean against an empty wall and stare at the floor until the bell rings.

We're doing a DNA experiment in health with strawberries and wheat germ and beakers, which makes it feel like science, even though it's not.

Benny and I collect our materials and follow the instructions.

I finish pouring the strawberry mixture through cheesecloth into our beaker when Benny leans in closer to me and whispers, "I saw Asha last night."

I look up at him, and through my cloudy goggles, I can tell he's happy about whatever happened, or at least he's not sad.

"I'm not supposed to get my hopes up when she's in the treatment center, because it's not the real world and anything can happen, but she made a joke, and it was funny. I laughed. I guess it sounds kind of stupid now that I'm saying it out loud."

"It doesn't. It sounds important."

"Thanks." He grins. "My parents have some special meeting with the clinic this afternoon, so I'm going to stay and watch your game, unless you think I shouldn't. I mean, is Emilia really mad that I said no?"

"What do you mean?" I ask, like I'm confused, because I am.

"She asked me out," he says. "Like to go out. But I said no."

"Really? When?"

"Uh, Saturday."

"Oh," I say, realizing that's what made Emilia extra mad at me.

"Wait, how do you not know this? Aren't you friends?"

I look down at my paper. "Not anymore."

"Shoot. Sorry. I forgot."

I want to ask him what he heard, but I don't. I measure the ethanol into a clean beaker and mix it with the strawberry solution. "It's fine. I mean, it's not, but it's my fault. I messed up." I hold up the beaker so we can see the white layer appear and the DNA start to become visible. "So, wait, why did you say no? I thought you wanted to be BF-GF with her."

"Who told you that?"

I shrug. "Not sure." Because even though Emilia is done being friends with me, I'm not going to say anything bad about her to Benny.

"I mean, Emilia's really cool," he says. "I just don't like her like that."

"Oh," I say. I don't want Benny to not like Emilia or for her to be hurt. It doesn't feel good that she lost. I don't feel like I won.

At lunch, I get food, then go to the library and read. Ryan has a meeting with her math teacher, and I don't have anyone else to sit with in the cafeteria. I'm not really that hungry, even though I didn't eat breakfast. I guess at some point between classes that empty feeling in my stomach disappeared.

Since no one is watching me, I eat half my apple and all the turkey, tomato, and lettuce from my sandwich. I pack up the bread because we have a game and I might need a bite later. I wait to feel hungry again and to need more food, but I don't feel anything for the rest of the day.

When the bell rings, I change into my uniform. I haven't seen Emilia once today, not in the hallway between classes or in the bathroom, and after what Benny told me in health, I'm nervous as soon as I step onto the court. I keep waiting for her to say something rude to me in front of everyone. But she doesn't. Instead, she pretends I'm not there. She doesn't pass to me during warm-ups, even when she's supposed to.

She acts like she can't see me. I'm invisible. It's worse.

The gym is starting to fill up with parents and siblings. Mom and Mrs. Martin are sitting next to each other, like always. Benny and Duke are here too, in the front.

I don't start, but Coach Lemon puts me in for Tamar pretty early in the game, and I end up playing most of the first two quarters. I'm on fire, making my shots, grabbing all the rebounds, and setting up my teammates with great passes. I forgot what it felt like to be on the court just to win. Not to prove something. Or be someone. It's fast and physical and in a weird way it's completely effortless. We're all moving together in sync. *Thump. Thump. Thump.* I know where to be without thinking too hard. Like a dance, but the choreography isn't set. It's all improv and instinct. My reflexes kick in. And I'm faster than ever.

By the start of the third quarter, there's energy pumping through me, making me jittery, like the time Dad let me try a few sips of his coffee.

I see my opening. *I've got this!* I steal the ball and sprint toward the right side of the basket, because I want to go in for a right-handed layup. There are no defenders between me and the hoop. No one to get in my way or hold me back. I push myself, running and dribbling as fast as I can. When I get to the basket, I jump off my left foot to make the layup and score. Only before I can get the ball into the hoop, my calf cramps up and my leg buckles under me. It's limp and floppy, like spaghetti. My body flails. The ball flies out of my hands. I fall under the basket and hit the floor.

The whistle blows.

I hear sneakers squeaking. Everyone stops. They're all standing in place, staring at me, in a pile on the floor.

"Sarah!" Mom shouts. "Sarah!"

I need to get up. It doesn't matter that I'm embarrassed and that I missed the shot. It was one mistake. I have to get back in the game.

Only I can't move. My left leg is cramping. I keep my eyes closed and wait until the pulsing finally stops and the pain is gone, and then I sit up. I'm light-headed and dizzy.

Ryan is standing over me. She kneels down. "Sarah, come on. You've got this."

I push my hands against the floor to pick myself up. But nothing happens. My body is heavy and I'm too tired.

"You're good to go." Ryan is holding both hands out to me. "Let's do this."

I take a deep breath and try to reach for her, but my hands are stuck to the floor. "I can't," I say. "I need help."

She bends down and pulls me up off the court.

I wrap my arm around her shoulder and lean against her, because I'm afraid if I don't, I might fall over again.

The ref walks toward us. "Everything okay, girls?"

The room is spinning, and there are shiny twinkling stars everywhere I turn. I grab on to Ryan. I can't let the ref know how bad I feel. I manage to look at her and nod.

"Okay. Good," she says, and nods back, believing me.

From where we're standing at the far end of the court, the bench seems miles away, and I'm not sure how we're ever going to get there.

"Don't let go." Ryan's voice is sharp, like a chef's knife on a cutting board.

"I won't," I say, but my words come out soft and small. It sounds like only part of me is here. I don't know where the rest went or how to get it back.

My arms are drenched in sweat. They're wet and slippery pressed up against Ryan, but she doesn't pull away. Her grip is firm and steady. She's not letting go. And even though I wish I could disappear, because I'm so embarrassed that everyone saw me mess up, it feels good that Ryan has my back.

I'm not sure how long it takes us to get to the sidelines. It feels like forever. But it can't actually be that long, because if it were taking a while, Coach Lemon or the ref would have come over to help us.

When we finally get to the bench, everyone starts clapping, as if I did something worthy of applause, when I didn't. I fell. I get that clapping is a thing people do because of sportsmanship or whatever, but I messed up and missed my shot and let my team down, so it doesn't give me warm fuzzies inside. It feels like they're rubbing it in.

"Sarah, honey." Mom is standing next to me now. Her forehead is crinkled up into a million little folds. She's looking at me, checking to see that all the different parts of me are still in place. "Are you okay?"

"I'm fine." I try my best to smile at her.

She takes a breath. "Okay."

The gym is a beehive, buzzing with hums and whispers.

I sink onto the bench, slouch down, and cover my face with both hands. All I want to do is hide.

Ryan stays next to me, still squeezing my arm, like she's afraid to let go, and I guess I'm sort of afraid of that too. It feels a little like she's holding me together.

Coach Lemon crouches down next to me and rests her hand lightly on my shoulder. "How are you, Sarah?" Her voice sounds softer than usual.

My eyes start to burn. I push everything I'm feeling inside. I can't cry in the middle of a game. I swallow. "I'm sorry I missed the shot. I don't know what happened. I thought I had it. But I'm ready to go back in now." I try to sound confident. I need Coach to put me in the game. I'm finally playing like myself, and everything is back to the way it should be.

I can feel Ryan's grip on my arm getting tighter, like she's silently yelling at me. It hurts. But I don't turn away from Coach Lemon.

"You played hard out there, Sarah, and I know you gave this game your all. You should be very proud. But you fell hard—"

"I know it looked bad, but it wasn't. I'm fine. Really. I'm ready to help the team." I sound desperate.

"I can't let you do that. You're sitting out for the rest of the game. That's my final decision. And you played a lot today. Please hydrate and have some orange slices." She points to the container under the bench.

I try to come up with a reason to make her change her mind, because I know playing basketball is the only thing that will help me feel better right now, but she isn't asking what I think, and before I can say anything else, she's walking over to the ref. I wish I could rewind to before I fell and missed that shot.

There's a dull pain behind my eyes. I barely have enough energy to hold my head up. I'm not sure I could play right now, even if she'd let me.

Ryan lets go of my arm. She reaches under the bench to get a water and the box of oranges and hands both to me. I take two slices, because Ryan is watching and one slice doesn't seem like enough, then I put the spout up to my mouth and drink as much water as I can.

When the ref blows the whistle, Ryan looks me over, like she's making a list. Then she gets up and walks back onto the court.

The game restarts exactly where it stopped. Only I've been replaced by Sage. I want to look up and watch and cheer for my team, but my eyes are heavy.

The oranges are slimy and sticky between my fingers. I keep my hand balled up in a fist, like I'm about to perform magic and make them disappear so I won't have to eat them, because I still don't know if I can. I never asked Mom, and I'm pretty sure I shouldn't, because she doesn't buy oranges, and they feel juicy, like they're all sugar, so I'm not doing it. I can't. Not now, when everything is already so messed up.

The buzzer sounds at the end of the game. I don't need to look up at the board to know we lost. But I can't stop myself: 31–30.

The girls on the opposite side of the court are cheering and smiling. That's what we would be doing if I'd made that layup and we'd won. I didn't just mess up for myself. I ruined the game for our team.

I pull myself off the bench, stand in line, and shake hands. I say *good game* over and over, even though it was the worst game of my life.

In the locker room, no one even whispers. There are no happy noises. It's just the sound of people trying to get away as fast as possible—zippers opening and closing and metal doors slamming shut. I keep my head down and collect my bags, while Ryan goes to the bathroom. When I look up again, the room is empty, and Ryan is standing in front of me with swollen eyes and a splotchy face, like she's been crying. It surprises me, because Ryan hardly ever cries. "Are you okay?" I ask.

"No." Her voice is steady, but she keeps sniffling, reminding me she's sad.

"Did something else happen with your brothers?"
She shakes her head. "I'm upset about you."

"I'm fine, Ry. Really," I say. "Promise."

"You're not. I know you're not eating enough. And I don't get why."

"I'm doing what I need to do to be good at basketball."

Ryan blinks. "That doesn't make any sense. Starving yourself is not going to make you better at anything."

"I'm not starving myself," I say. "I'm being healthy."

"Then why didn't you eat the orange slices?"

"Because I don't know if they're good for me."

"What are you talking about? Oranges are fruit! They're obviously good for you," she says.

"Not all fruit is healthy," I say back.

"Um, yes, it is. It comes from the earth."

"So what? Mangoes come from the earth, and they're really bad for you. They're all sugar. They're like candy. Bananas have a lot of calories. And I'm not sure about oranges, so I didn't eat them."

"Nothing you just said is true. I don't know who told you any of that, but they're wrong. Like really, really wrong."

"My mom! So, no, actually she's not wrong. She's my mom and an adult, and I'm pretty sure she knows more than you do."

"She doesn't!" Ryan shouts. "Your mom is the worst

about food. I hate going to your house. There's never enough to eat. And even when there is, it's like no one is allowed to. She makes it seem like food is so bad, and you can tell she judges people by what they eat. I swear she was counting my pizza slices at our sleepover. I'm hungry the entire time I'm at your house, because I'm afraid to say I'm hungry and have her look at me like it's so shocking. I'm sorry if it's rude or the wrong thing to say, but your mom is not someone to look to for healthy eating habits. I've never seen her eat anything except candy. She doesn't know about being healthy."

I feel like I just got punched in the face. "You can't say that. And you can't just tell me not to trust her. She's my mom."

Ryan takes a deep breath. "I know," she says. "I'm sorry. It's not fair that she doesn't feed you like she should. But you still have to eat."

"I eat. The rules about food are different for girls like me. You don't get it yet. Everything is the same for you. But I can't eat too much or the wrong things, or my body will change again, and then I'll be slow and bad at basketball."

"That's not true," she says. "Do you even hear what you're saying right now? Basketball players have all different bodies. You need to be strong to dominate on the court."

"I'm not strong. I'm fast, and I can make any shot. That's what I'm good at. But I can't score if I'm never open, and I'm not going back to how I was at the beginning of the season. So, no. Just, no."

"You don't have enough energy to make it through half a game."

"I do," I say, even though I'm sort of afraid she's right.

"You didn't see yourself fall. It looked like your body gave up on you. It was really bad, Sarah. And it could have been a lot worse. You could have hit your head. You might, if it happens again."

I swallow hard. "It won't. I'm fine."

She shakes her head. "I don't think so. That stuff you said about fruit is really messed up and sort of scary actually. Your mom—"

"Stop talking about my mom!" I shout. "You don't know anything about her. Don't act like you do." I'm not sure why I'm so mad at Ryan for saying the things I already know about Mom, but they sound a lot worse coming out of her mouth.

"I don't care what your mom does or eats or doesn't eat. I just don't want her to mess things up for you."

"She's not."

"I think you need to talk to Coach Lemon and tell her what you're doing."

"What are you talking about? I'm not doing anything. Why would I talk to Coach Lemon?"

"Because you need help."

"No. I don't," I say. "I already told you I'm fine."

"You're not. And if you don't talk to her, then I'm going to."

"What? No. Ryan, come on. Don't do that. You can't do that to me."

Ryan doesn't say anything. She just stands there staring at me, like she's waiting for me to change my mind and say it's okay for her to talk to Coach Lemon, but it's not.

"You get that tattling on me is going to hurt the team, right? Then we definitely won't win the championship or make the Hall of Fame."

"You're my best friend. I care way more about you eating enough and actually being healthy than I do about the Hall of Fame." Her face is all scrunched up, and her eyes are watery.

I can't stop the tears from falling down my face, because I want to believe her—that it's more important for me to eat than to be good at basketball. And I know I'm supposed to. But it doesn't feel possible.

Ryan sniffles. "You need help from someone who isn't messed up about food."

Dad is good at food. And he agreed with Mom that I'm healthy. So I'm fine. "I don't need to talk to Coach Lemon," I say.

"I'm going to see her at lunch tomorrow. If you're not there, I'm telling her anyway." Then Ryan picks up her bags and storms out, letting the heavy door slam shut.

I need to catch up with Ryan and beg her to not tell Coach Lemon, but by the time I book it out of the locker room, she's already outside in the car, and her mom is driving away. I just lost the only person in the world who was on my side.

Mom is standing by herself, waiting for me. As soon as I'm next to her, she pulls me in and kisses my forehead. "I've never seen you fall like that, honey. You scared me."

"Sorry," I say. "I guess I didn't eat enough today." I don't know why I tell Mom, but as soon as the words are out, I know they're true.

"Really?"

"Yeah. There wasn't anything to eat for breakfast, and I didn't have that much for lunch. Some turkey and an apple."

"Hmm." Mom nods like she's listening, but I'm not sure

my words are getting in, because she says, "Well, I'm glad you're okay."

"Did you hear what I said?" I ask.

"Yes, honey, I heard you. You don't think you ate enough and that's why you fell." The way she says it back to me makes it seem like it's my opinion, instead of a fact, and she's looking at me like she doesn't see a problem, like there isn't one. Mom doesn't seem worried at all.

"What are we having for dinner?" I ask.

"I didn't have time to get to the store today," she says. "But we have leftover soup and chicken. We'll figure it out at home."

Only I don't believe her. There isn't any chicken left. My stomach hurts thinking about the soup and the smell of our fridge. "Can we please stop at the store on the way home? The chicken is gone, and we don't have anything for breakfast either."

Mom sighs. It's the big, loud kind that echoes off the walls and back at me. "Fine." Only the way she says it makes it seem like it's not okay at all.

"Really? Are you sure?" Because even though I know we need food, I feel bad for asking. It makes me wish I weren't hungry. And I realize I'm asking Mom about dinner to prove that Ryan is wrong and that I can trust Mom, even when it comes to food. But it's not working.

"Yes. We can stop on the way." Mom looks at my bags. "Let me help you."

"I've got it," I say.

"You worked hard in the game, and you had a big fall, sweetheart. You must be tired." She takes my backpack and swings it over her shoulder, then pries my basketball bag from my hand and carries my stuff to our car. She acts like the problem is just that I'm too tired to carry my bags, when deep down, I know it's so much bigger than that.

TEN

AT BREAKFAST, I mix salted almond butter into my yogurt. It tastes gross, but that doesn't change the fact that I have to eat it. I need to do everything possible to make sure my leg doesn't cramp up again in practice today. And last night when I searched my phone for ways to avoid leg cramps, it said to drink water and eat bananas. Only we don't have any. It also said to eat food with salt, and salted almond butter was the only salt I could find in our house.

My stomach starts to feel bloated about halfway through the yogurt, and I get nervous that if I eat more than normal, I won't be able to play my best, so I stop.

At school, I can't find Ryan. She isn't in the lobby or

the bathroom or the gym. So I text her: **Can we talk?**

She doesn't write back.

I'm not sure if she's avoiding me because of our fight, or if something else is going on, but it seems like she's always late for school now.

Ryan and I don't have any classes together. I won't have a chance to see her before lunch and stop her from talking to Coach Lemon, which means I have to get to the office first and explain that what happened in the game was not a big deal. I actually think it's pretty rude of Ryan to say something is wrong with me when there are people like Benny's sister who are really sick and I'm not.

After the lunch bell rings, I sprint across the hall and down two flights of stairs. By the time I get to Coach Lemon's office, I'm sweating. Ryan is already there.

I think about walking away and letting her say whatever she wants about me. I don't even know why we're here. I mean, I guess it's because Ryan thinks Mom's rules are wrong. And she's telling on me no matter what I do, so I need to be here to defend myself.

I walk into the office, close the door behind me, and sit down in the empty chair next to Ryan.

"What can I do for you, girls?" Coach Lemon smiles, like

we're a welcome surprise, which means Ryan hasn't said anything about me yet.

"I don't think you can do anything," I say. "But Ryan is making me talk to you."

"Okay," Coach Lemon says. "I'm listening."

Neither of us speaks. We stew in the awkward silence. I can tell Ryan is waiting for me to talk, but I didn't ask for this meeting. She did.

Ryan clears her throat. "Sarah didn't eat enough yesterday. That's why she fell."

I cringe. "You don't actually know that."

"Yes, I do."

"That's just your opinion. My mom had a different one."

"Do you want to tell me what you ate?" Coach Lemon asks.

"I guess." I cross my arms over my chest. "I had most of an apple, and a turkey sandwich without the bread."

Her eyebrows knit together. "That isn't enough food, Sarah."

"But you said we need less food once we're adults. And I'm definitely more of an adult than Ryan."

"*I* said that?"

"Yes," I say. "In health."

Coach Lemon's eyes get wide. "Just to be clear, in case I

wasn't before, regardless of whether you are a kid or adult, growing or not, you need to listen to your body first and foremost, rather than guess how much food you *think* you should need."

"I can't do that," I say. "I need to be good at basketball. That's the whole reason I started eating less and following other rules from my mom and the list from the packet you handed out in class."

"What rules are you talking about?" Coach Lemon asks.

"The rules of being healthy," I say.

"Could you tell me about the rules that feel important to you?"

"They're all important."

"Okay. Maybe you can give me a few examples?"

"Sure," I say. I can just say these rules and Coach Lemon will see that I'm actually being healthy, and then Ryan will know I'm right and she's wrong. "No bananas or mangoes or juice or—" I stop myself. "It's probably easier for me to list the good foods than to tell you everything bad and sometimes bad."

"Let's back up for a minute. Why do you have to follow any rules?"

"I told you. I'm being healthy for basketball. And I mean, I don't exactly have a choice when I'm home. We don't have a lot of options, like I wanted a banana this morning so I wouldn't get a leg cramp again today, but we don't have any because they have a lot of calories and sugar. My mom is really healthy. That's why we don't have carbs or starchy foods with dinner or too many snacks."

Coach Lemon nods. "I can see you're trying to be mindful of what you eat. There can be a lot of pressure, especially at your age. Have you ever gone more than a day without food?"

"Not a whole day. Sometimes my mom forgets dinner." I don't know why I say it. "But that doesn't happen all the time or anything. Just once in a while."

"She does?" Ryan sounds surprised.

"Yeah." I look down at my hands.

"How often do you think that happens?" Coach Lemon asks.

"I've never counted. It feels like it's always about to happen. And it doesn't help to talk to my mom about food, if that's what you're going to say next. I've tried. That makes things worse."

"I understand," she says, but I really don't think she does. "Does your mom ever forget anything else? Does she ever forget to pick you up from school?"

"No," I say. "She would never do that. She's only missed one of my basketball games ever, like in my life. And that was for work. She didn't want to."

"What about your safety? Have you ever been hurt by anyone at home?"

Whoa. Why would she ask me that? "No. I told you, my mom just wants us to be healthy and watch what we eat."

"It's not healthy to have no food in your house," Ryan blurts out.

"Stop." I look at her. "You don't get to be mad. No one ever forgets to make you dinner."

"Sorry." Ryan slumps into her chair.

"That must be hard," Coach Lemon says.

"I guess." My words come out muffled.

"Sarah, you know, it's okay to be upset."

"Yeah, I know," I say. "But this is not that big of a deal."

"It sounds like a big deal to me. Food is a way we take care of people we love. So, when your mom forgets about dinner or there isn't enough to eat, that must hurt."

I shrug. "It didn't use to be like this. Or maybe it just didn't bother me, because I always felt good after practice. I knew for sure that at least I mattered to the team."

"You *do* matter to the team," she says.

"I do now. But I didn't before. I only started to matter again when I stopped eating so much."

"That's not true," she sputters. "I've been coaching for a long time, and I know a lot about teen athletes trying to put off puberty by not eating enough, because it's a common problem."

What? It is?

She says, "If I didn't think you could succeed at basketball in the way I know you want to, I'd be encouraging you to reset your expectations. But you're a strong player. You just can't be your best in basketball or anything else if you aren't eating."

"It was working. I got faster and better. I was back to my old self."

"That energy you got from not eating at first was adrenaline. It's the body's way of reacting to hunger, so that in caveman days, you'd have the energy to find food. It's temporary. Eventually if you don't eat enough, your muscles break down."

Oh. Wow. I definitely didn't know that. "So, I need to eat enough that my body doesn't break down, but not so much that it starts changing again?"

"That's absolutely not what I'm saying." Coach Lemon takes a deep breath.

"Then I don't get what you expect me to do. I can't lose basketball."

"You won't," she says.

"I almost did."

"That's not how I saw the situation. And I think we can all agree that I know a lot more about basketball than you do."

I nod, because she definitely does.

"The link you've created between basketball and food doesn't exist. The real link is between basketball and puberty. And puberty is going to happen no matter what you eat. You just slowed it down temporarily. But once you get through this stage, a lot of your coordination and athleticism will come back and I know you'll keep pushing yourself to improve. Every single player you see in college and the WNBA went through this too. You have so much potential, and a lot of impressive parts of your game."

"Like what?" I ask.

"You think on your feet. You know how to get yourself in the right position. You're a leader and a team player at the same time, which is rare."

I wish I could record everything Coach Lemon just said in my mind, so I could replay it whenever I start to forget about the good parts of me, when the bad things feel so big they overpower everything else. "You really think I'm all those things?"

"I do," she says. "But I can see you're having a hard time feeling good about yourself."

I swallow. "Yeah," I say, because she's right about that. "But isn't that like a middle school thing or whatever?"

"It can be. You're going through a lot of changes and that's hard. But it's even harder when your basic needs aren't being met at home and when the ground you're standing on doesn't always feel safe."

"It mostly does," I say.

"That's not good enough," Ryan says.

It feels like "mostly" should be enough for me. And like there's something wrong with me that it isn't. Maybe I'm the one who needs to change. "It's really not as bad as I made it seem."

"Yes, it is," Ryan says. "When I stay at your house, I expect to be hungry. I can't wait to leave. I get why it seems normal to you, but it's not, and it's starting to mess up the way you see everything—like even yourself."

"So what? There's nothing I can do. My parents aren't going to change."

"I want to try to make things better for you," Coach Lemon says. "You deserve to have enough food at home."

"I really don't see how that's ever going to happen."

"I'd like to start by having you and your parents meet with Ms. Varna."

"The school counselor?" I ask.

"She's great at helping everyone get on the same page. It'll give your family a chance to hear what you need."

I think about what Coach Lemon just said for a few seconds, and how it could be easier to talk to Mom and Dad if an adult who is a professional at this kind of thing were there to help me. "I guess it's worth a shot."

"That's great," Coach Lemon says. "I'd also like for you to meet with Ms. Varna on your own."

"Why?" I ask.

"I think it might help if you had someone to talk to about how you're feeling."

"But I don't have a real problem."

"Me neither," Ryan says. "But I started talking to Ms. Varna when all this college stuff happened with my brothers."

"You did? I mean, I knew you were upset, especially after UNC. I'm sorry. I had no clue it was that bad for you."

"It wasn't at first. I used to go once in a while to vent, like at lunch or before school if I was having a bad day. But then after they got offers from big schools, I started going every week, sometimes more. I've been really angry and sad about the fact that I don't count as much because I'm a girl. It helps to talk."

"But like how? I don't see how it could help me."

"I guess because you can say what's wrong and figure out why it bothers you. I mean, there's nothing anyone can do to fix my situation either. No one is going to change the world so that the WNBA counts as much as the NBA. But Ms. Varna listens to me talk about how unfair that feels when I'm with my family and she takes me seriously and then what they think just doesn't matter as much to me."

I don't know why, but hearing that Ryan sees Ms. Varna makes it seem like less of a big deal and more like meeting with a teacher after class for extra help, only for life instead of for homework. "Okay," I say. "I'll try."

Coach Lemon lets out a deep breath and smiles, like she's relieved. I want to feel that too. I want to be able to let go of all the fear and pain I've been holding inside.

"There's one more thing, Sarah. The school has a policy for coaches that if a student comes to us with symptoms of an eating disorder, we're required to report the conversation to the counselor and the student has to sit out of practice until we have approval for them to participate. I don't think this policy is fair. I don't like how it can make students feel less inclined to ask for help in the future, but I have to follow the rule, because it's part of my job."

My eyes fill with tears.

"I didn't know that was going to happen." Ryan leans in and rubs my shoulder, and I let her, because I know she didn't.

"Please don't take basketball away from me," I say.

"That's the last thing I want to do," Coach Lemon says.

"But I don't, like, have an actual problem. It's not *that* serious."

"Sarah, I've heard you say a few times today that you don't have a problem. I want to be clear—that's not how I see the situation. Everything you're going through sounds very serious to me."

The room is blurry, and I can't stop crying, because it feels good to hear her say that what I'm going through is hard. It makes me think about all the times I felt like I didn't matter and how I thought that's what I deserved—and it hurts so much.

"Thanks for thinking my problems are a big deal," I say.

"Thank you for trusting me to help you. We'll get you back to playing basketball and feeling good on the court as fast as we can."

Before we leave, Coach Lemon calls Ms. Varna.

And it's good news! She can meet with me first thing tomorrow, which means I only have to miss one practice.

Ryan and I don't say anything to each other on our walk to the cafeteria. We get our food and sit down at an empty table by the door. I unwrap my sandwich, and then drink half my water bottle out of habit. Ryan's pizza smells good, and I keep thinking about how great it would be to eat her lunch instead of my plain turkey sandwich.

"I think it's cool that you showed up today," Ryan says between bites. "It must have been hard to say all that stuff out loud."

"Yeah. But it was kind of good too. I just don't want to have to say everything again to Ms. Varna."

"It'll be different," she says. "New things will come up."

"Uh, that doesn't make me feel better."

"I mean, yeah, it's scary to say things you don't want to, but it's like talking makes the hard stuff easier. I've really learned that from Ms. Varna."

I nod and try as hard as I can to believe her. I eat my sandwich—one bite at a time. I want to show myself I can be okay. It tastes so much better with the bread. But after I finish, I'm full and uncomfortable. And it feels a lot harder to trust Coach Lemon—that I can eat food I like and also be good at basketball—than it does to just eat less. I want to tell Ryan everything I'm thinking, but I don't know how, so I say, "I'm really scared."

She grabs my hand. "Coach Lemon said a lot of people have this problem. That means there are adults who will know how to help. Just hang on, okay?"

I squeeze back. "Okay," I say. And I don't let go until the bell rings.

After school, I don't change for practice. I stay in my regular clothes and stand next to Coach Lemon on the court, watching my teammates run drills. Dad says you can learn a lot from observing other players and I think that's probably true, because Mom knows so much about hoops from just watching. I stay focused on Ines and a few other girls who aren't always fast but are strong and strategic, and track the ways they help our team.

No one asks why I'm sitting out or says anything rude to

my face, because I'm standing next to Coach Lemon. But Emilia keeps leaning over and whispering things to Ryan. I'm pretty sure she's asking questions about me. I do my best to ignore her, because I know Ryan won't answer. But even if she told Emilia the truth, Coach Lemon already knows about my problems. And it's nice that for once I don't have anything to hide.

ELEVEN

WHEN I GET TO Ms. Varna's office in the morning, she says, "Come on in, Sarah." She's not the smiling type, but her voice is soft and welcoming, like a fancy doorbell.

I told Mom I had to be at school early for a group project. Coach Lemon might think that what I'm going through is a big deal, but Mom won't. No chance.

Ms. Varna's office smells like cinnamon tea. There are framed photographs and hand-drawn sketches in a gallery on the wall. I sit down and tug on my belt loops and my shirt, adjusting myself, but no matter how hard I push and pull on my clothes, I can't get comfortable. I don't lean back. I sit at the edge of my chair.

Ms. Varna takes a sip from her mug. Her lips are glossy, and she's wearing a deep purple dress that's bright and pretty against her brown skin and makes her shine even more than usual. She stands up, bringing her notebook with her, then sits down next to me. Ms. Varna fills up the chair. The arms on either side hug her waist, but she doesn't rearrange her clothing, the way I do, like she's comfortable in her body, in her office, in the world. I wish I could be like that.

"Coach Lemon filled me in on what you talked about yesterday," Ms. Varna says.

"Oh," I say. But I shouldn't be surprised. Teachers are always "updating" each other, which is basically talking behind our backs, but it's allowed, because they're adults and in charge of us.

"How do you feel about being here today?"

I twist a strand of my half-wet, half-dry hair. The ends feel crispy and frozen between my fingers. "Um, I guess nervous that nothing is going to help. And I don't know what to do, because before, I was afraid to eat too much and the wrong things, since that was holding me back in basketball, but Coach Lemon won't let me play unless I eat enough. So, now I'm afraid to eat and I'm afraid to not eat."

"That sounds overwhelming."

"Yeah," I say. "It is."

"Could you tell me what it would mean if you weren't able to play basketball?"

I flinch. "No. It's who I am."

"It's something you like and one way you define yourself, but it's not who you are. You're many things."

"None of those other things are important. Except for cooking, and I just started learning how, so I'm not like the best yet or anything, but I like it."

"Me too." Ms. Varna smiles. "What do you like to cook?"

"So far, salmon. I want to try making other kinds of fish too. But I'm never going to be the best, because I can't practice at home." I fiddle with my hair again. "Even if Benny and I get picked for Chef Junior, I'm not sure it's ever going to feel that great to me. My mom is weird about food. She wouldn't like it if I were good at cooking."

"Does she like that you're good at basketball?" Ms. Varna asks.

"Definitely. She loves the sport. Plus, it's healthy and exercise."

"Hmm." Ms. Varna pauses for a few seconds, like she's

thinking. "What do you mean when you say your mom is weird about food?"

"Just that we never have a lot of food in our house, except candy and cookies."

"I imagine those foods feel safe to your mom?"

Huh, I never thought about that. "I guess."

"Do you have foods that feel safe?"

"Um, yeah—yogurt, apples, turkey, chicken, fish, vegetables."

"What about foods that feel threatening?"

"Everything else." I look at the floor. It sounds worse out loud than in my head.

"I'm sorry. That must be hard."

I shrug.

"I'd like to help you feel good about eating every kind of food."

That's never going to happen. "No offense, but I'm pretty sure that's impossible."

"That's not offensive. It's honest. And I always want you to be honest with me. That's the only way I'll be able to help you." She's looking at me like she really wants to make things better. "I know being able to eat all types of food feels far away, but it is possible."

"Do you know what's wrong with me that I can't be normal about food?" I ask. "I'm not sick. I don't have an eating disorder. But I'm not regular or like everyone else."

"There's no such thing," she says.

"Okay. Fine. But you know what I mean."

"The reason you're struggling probably doesn't have very much to do with food, other than the fact that you're afraid to eat and you also need to eat."

"That doesn't make sense. I think about food all the time." I really don't get what else it could be about.

"You don't want to think about who you are without basketball, so instead you've been spending your time controlling what you eat to be good at basketball and to avoid facing how you feel about yourself. And I think you deserve to feel like you're enough on your own, regardless of what you eat or if you play basketball."

Everything Ms. Varna just said sounds like it could be true, and I really want to believe her, because she seems sure of herself and she makes me feel like I could be that way too.

"I want you to work on changing how you're thinking about food as good and bad."

"But like some food is actually bad," I say. "Like Twinkies and pepperoni and muffins and butter."

"No," she says. "Food doesn't have a moral value."

"So, it's fine to eat potato chips all day?"

"There's room for all types of food, including potato chips. But our bodies like variety. We need different nutrients and vitamins so we don't get sick. I think you'll find if you only eat potato chips, you won't want them anymore."

She's wrong. She has to be. "Just so you know, this is the opposite of what everyone else thinks."

"Who do you mean when you say 'everyone else'?"

"Literally everyone calls chips junk food." I shift in my seat. "But then, also, my friend Emilia said diets make people gain a lot of weight. So basically I'm doomed. I mean, I already messed myself up."

"Your body is not messed up, Sarah. And it wasn't before. It's doing everything right."

"But she said it's a fact, like from her doctor—diets ruin people's bodies."

Ms. Varna looks right at me, and I don't turn away. "You're not ruined."

I nod and try to let her words sink all the way in.

"It would be a lot easier if there was one right way to eat," she says. "But we're too complicated for an instruction manual. Our bodies tell us what we need, and we have to listen."

"What about the foods I'm only supposed to eat in moderation?" I ask.

"You should eat those foods too, if you like them," she says. "And if you eat a little more than you need, because you're happy or you're celebrating or it tastes good, your body will recalibrate."

"Okay." I nod. "I guess that makes sense."

"When you have a negative thought about food, I want you to say to yourself—*All foods are allowed*. It's going to be hard at first. But it will get easier. Eventually I'd like you to get to the point where what you eat doesn't take up so much space in your head or define how you feel about yourself."

"I want that too," I say. "I'm afraid food is always going to be hard for me."

"You can change."

I try to trust her. "What about basketball? Can I practice tomorrow?"

"I'd really like us to meet with your parents first so we can come up with a plan. But I know how important basketball is to you, and I promise I will do everything possible to schedule this meeting for the morning so you can practice."

"Okay," I say. "Thanks."

When I leave Ms. Varna's office, Ryan is standing in the hall with girls from the team. As soon as she sees me, she leaves their circle and walks over, like I'm more important to her than everyone else put together.

"How'd it go?" she asks.

"Pretty good. You were right."

She exhales and smiles.

"But I can't practice until we have a plan with my parents. We're probably talking to them tomorrow."

"That makes sense," she says. "I covered for you, because you know, um, people were talking. I said you were kind of sick and that's why you couldn't practice, so maybe act tired in class or something."

"What were they saying?"

"You don't want to know."

I take a deep breath and stand up a little taller, because I know I can handle whatever they said about me. "Yeah. I do. Please tell me."

"Emilia said you're not eating to get attention, so everyone should ignore you and not give you what you want."

I breathe in. "Wow."

"She's being so rude. But not everyone agreed with her. I just doubt the sick thing will go over if you don't play again since, you know, you're in school."

"Yeah," I say. "Probably not."

"I'm sorry. It's my fault you can't practice."

"Don't," I say. "You helped. And I need help."

Ryan hugs me.

I hug her back.

"We'll think up a good excuse," she says. "Everything is going to be fine."

And for the first time in forever, I actually believe that's true.

Benny walks over to me at dismissal, because his mom is picking me up and taking me to their house so we can practice for Chef Junior. Mom sent in a note to give me permission to go home with him. But now that it's happening and Tamar and Sage and Emilia and everyone else can see us leave school together, it feels like a way bigger deal in real life than it did in my head.

When I get in the car, Benny's mom smiles and points to the snacks on the seat next to me, and then goes back to her phone conversation. The other person, a man, who I think is Benny's dad, is on speaker. They're talking in Farsi, so I'm not sure what they're saying, but I can tell by the way their voices swing up that they're happy.

Benny is looking at his mom, hanging on to her every word. I really hope it's good news about Asha.

I look at the snacks—Goldfish, pretzels, Doritos.

I pick Doritos. I want them. I miss the crunch and the cheesy flavor. Only I haven't had them in a few weeks, and I'm not sure how I'll feel after I eat them, so I don't open the bag. It's too big of a risk. I want to feel confident while we cook. I put the Doritos back down. Maybe I'll have some tomorrow. I take an apple out of my bag and eat that for now.

Once we're at Benny's house, we go straight into the kitchen and work together to get everything ready. We split the list of ingredients down the middle. I search his pantry and fridge collecting all the different things we need to make shepherd's pie. They have so much food. I really want my house to be like this too.

I set up our stations while Benny finds the pots and pans and tools.

It's by far the hardest recipe we've tried. There are a lot of steps. Everything has to be prepped and cooked separately, then layered and baked together. And we won't know how it's going to work out until the very end.

I dice the onion, rinsing my knife with cold water so my eyes don't tear up, and quarter the potatoes before boiling them. Then I soften the butter and measure the cream, getting the other ingredients ready, while Benny drains the potatoes.

When I'm cooking and food is in my hands, between my fingers, it feels different. I'm in charge of how the ingredients make me feel instead of the other way around.

I don't think about the butter wrapper or the cream. I'm supposed to be changing my thought pattern. *Every food is allowed.* I keep saying it over in my mind, because I trust Ms. Varna and Coach Lemon and Ryan. They're trying to help me. And I want to help me too. I don't feel good about myself. I'm not happy. And I want to be. I think I deserve to be.

I don't realize how focused I am on getting everything right until Benny sets the timer and puts the dish into the oven.

While we wait for the shepherd's pie to bake, I practice panfrying salmon, because it's really hard and I want to be great at it. I wait until the pan is hot, put the fish in skin-side down, and set a timer so I know how long it's been cooking, and then Benny shows me how to watch and look for signs that it's ready to be flipped, because every piece of fish is different, so the timer is only a guide. You need to listen and watch and trust your instincts. I practice over and over, and by the time the shepherd's pie is ready, I feel like I actually know what I'm doing.

Benny covers both his hands with mitts and takes the dish out. He paces while it cools. When it's finally ready, he puts out two plates, serves the shepherd's pie, and then takes a big bite, making sure to get all the layers at once.

"It tastes really good, but—" He points to the dish. "It's a mess."

I lean in closer to see for myself. The layer of potato is sagging. It looks sloppy and mushy. "Do you think that matters?"

"Not in regular life. But in Chef Junior . . ."

"True," I say. "It's part of the presentation."

"Try it," he says.

"One minute." I take my phone out of my bag. I'm not stalling this time. I'm problem solving. I search—*Why is my shepherd's pie watery?* Then scroll and scan through the results. There are a lot of comments about vegetables and meat and the sauce and broth, but those layers look perfect to me. They're sturdy and even. "It's the potatoes," I say. "Maybe we should have boiled them with the skin on and then taken the skin off, instead of taking it off before we boiled them."

"That's it." Benny is nodding. "Ugh. I thought the potatoes might be an issue, but I didn't know what to do."

"Next time, tell me about anything you think might go wrong with the recipe, and I can come up with solutions before we start cooking. I'm really good at puzzles."

"Oh yeah." He grins. "All those detective books."

I nod. "Exactly."

"I can't believe I forgot to tell you," he says. "I found this really cool graphic novel about these two detectives on a spaceship—*Sanity and Tallulah*. Want to borrow it after I'm done?"

"Um, yes! That sounds awesome." I pick up my fork and take a bite of the shepherd's pie. It's warm and comforting. "OMG! It's seriously so good!"

"I really think we can do this," Benny says.

"Me too," I say, because I know if we work together, we can make it onto the show.

TWELVE

THE NEXT MORNING, Mom, Dad, and I walk into school early. It's weird to be here when no one else is. It feels a little like we're breaking the rules. I can tell by the fact that the regular person isn't at the front desk that Ms. Varna pulled strings to make this meeting happen.

I'm not sure when she called my parents or what she told them, because Mom and Dad didn't say anything specific. They just told me we had to get to school first thing to speak with Ms. Varna, and I didn't ask questions, because I was nervous they'd start asking me questions back.

Ms. Varna is waiting for us in the lobby. "Good morning," she says to me. "Very nice to meet you both." She shakes hands with Mom and Dad, and then leads us down the long hall and around the corridor into her office.

We file in behind her and sit down.

Mom and Dad look stiff and nervous and sort of young, like they're in trouble, even though that's impossible, because they're adults and my parents.

"I'm glad you could make it on short notice," Ms. Varna says.

"Of course." Mom tucks her shiny hair behind her ears.

"Thank you for agreeing to schedule this so quickly," Dad says.

I keep reminding myself to breathe.

"As I mentioned to you over the phone"—Ms. Varna looks at Mom—"Sarah has been struggling to feel confident in herself, and now that we're together, I'd like to share more details about what she's been going through and come up with a plan for how we can work together to help support her."

Mom and Dad are both nodding a lot. Even though I'm nervous because they definitely don't know this meeting is about food yet, the way they're looking at Ms. Varna right now makes me feel like maybe they'll understand.

"Recently, Sarah has become preoccupied by food. She's been restricting what she eats and only eating foods that she's labeled healthy, in part because she wants to be faster in basketball."

Dad is squinting, like Ms. Varna is speaking a foreign language and he's trying to translate.

Mom looks like she's in shock.

It's silent for a few seconds. No one says anything.

Mom folds her arms over her chest, then clears her throat. "There's nothing wrong with wanting to be healthy, and Sarah isn't underweight."

As soon as Mom says I'm not *that* skinny, I can't stop myself from believing her. I wish I could erase certain things Mom says from my brain, because her words feel like facts, and they start to sink in and take over the way I see everything, even myself.

"Just to be clear, a person does not have to be underweight to be diagnosed with an eating disorder." Ms. Varna's voice is firm and a little louder than before. "And while Sarah is subclinical, she has disordered eating symptoms that are concerning to me."

"What do you mean by disordered eating symptoms?" Mom re-tucks her hair.

"I mean, irregular and problematic behaviors and patterns around food. It's compounded by the fact that her eating affects her basketball and her basketball affects her self-worth. So, it can feel like her eating affects her worth. That's a difficult cycle to break."

Dad puts his head in his hands. "I haven't been paying enough attention," he says softly, almost to himself. "And I should have been." He looks up at me. "I'm sorry."

I almost tell him it's okay, but I stop myself. I don't want to say something that isn't true. That's not going to help me get what I need. "Thanks," I say, because it does help to know that Dad never got how bad it was for me.

"What can we do now?" he asks Ms. Varna.

"Great question," she says. "Sarah needs help developing a flexible relationship with food, where all foods are allowed and her identity is based on more than her body image and ability in basketball. I can work with her on confidence and her feelings about self-worth, but my recommendation is for her to also meet with a therapist who specializes in eating disorders."

"I'm confused," Mom says. "Why would she need to talk to someone about an eating disorder if she doesn't have one?"

"If her symptoms aren't addressed, it's possible that eventually she might be diagnosed with one."

Mom shakes her head. "I just don't know if that's necessary at this point."

"When is it necessary?" My words come out way too loud. "I fell in the game, remember? Should we wait until I hit my head?"

"Of course not," Mom says. "I saw you fall. It was awful. But I'm not sure how you falling is related to this conversation."

"I fell because I didn't eat enough," I say.

"Oh," Mom says, putting the pieces together. "I didn't realize." I think about saying that I told her after the game but I don't, because I know she never remembers anything I say about food. "Well, now you know what happened so you can make sure you don't do that again."

"I can't!" I shout. "That's literally why we're here."

"I don't understand." Mom sighs. "Lots of people go on diets. It's not the same as having an eating disorder." She looks at Ms. Varna. "Don't we all have some kind of issue with food?"

"Not everyone. But you're right that many people

diet and have a problematic relationship with food and don't get support. But Sarah knows she can't handle her disordered eating on her own, and she's asking for help."

I take a deep breath, because Ms. Varna just said everything I've been thinking and feeling and having a hard time saying out loud, and I know for sure she's right and Mom is wrong.

Mom is staring straight ahead. I can't tell if she's really listening, and I need her to know what I'm going through. I realize the only way that's going to happen is if I tell her while Ms. Varna is here to back me up. "Mom, I'm not okay. I'm afraid to eat and I'm afraid to not eat. It doesn't help that we don't have enough food in our house."

"We have plenty of food, Sarah," Mom says. "Please, don't be dramatic."

Her words slam into me, and I can feel my heart break apart and then start to crumble into tiny pieces.

Ms. Varna looks at Mom. "Sarah is trying to tell you how she sees things. It's okay for you to have a different perspective, and even for you to need different things, but let's hold off on talking her out of her feelings, because they're real to her."

"Well, my perspective is that I try to make sure there's always a healthy dinner on the table. But I've been on a diet since I was eight. I was chubby, and that wasn't allowed. I never got sweets. That's all I ever wanted. For a while, that's all I ate. Sometimes I don't want to think about food, so I don't, and I forget to cook. I know I'm not perfect. But I'm doing my best."

I didn't know that about Mom.

"That sounds hard," Ms. Varna says.

"Yeah." Mom's eyes fall to the floor.

"It might help if you also met with a therapist. I have a few names of colleagues I can share."

"You think *I* need a therapist?" Mom is looking at Ms. Varna now. "For my own self?"

"I think therapy could help you and also give you tools to change how you address food with Sarah."

Mom doesn't say anything for a few seconds.

I'm scared she's going to say no.

She opens her mouth to answer, but I don't let her. "Please," I say. "Can't you please give it a chance?" I know that's what I need—for Mom to acknowledge that her problem with food is real, and so is mine. "I get that you're doing your best. But it's not good enough. You can't forget dinner. I already feel like I don't matter—"

"What do you mean you don't matter?" Mom asks.

"There's nothing to eat. And that makes me feel like I don't matter to you or deserve to be fed."

Mom is staring back at me. There are tears in her eyes. "What? Of course you matter to me. You matter so much, Sarah. I love you."

I'm crying, because right now I know she loves me. But I don't always. And I'm so tired of feeling like I only matter part of the time.

"I tried to do this better," Mom says. "This wasn't supposed to happen. It's obviously my fault that you're having these problems."

"It's really not," Ms. Varna says. "But you are one of the people Sarah relies on. She needs to feel safe with you no matter what she eats or how things go in basketball, and she doesn't. My concern is that your relationship with food might be making it hard for Sarah to be able to trust you."

"I didn't know I was hurting you." Mom is looking at me. "I'm so sorry."

"Liv," Dad says, "I could see someone too. I think we need to do whatever it takes."

Mom is quiet for a minute. Then she takes a deep breath

and looks at me. "Okay," she says. "I'll try therapy. I want to be someone you can trust."

And I know she means it. I lean in and hug Mom. "Thank you. I love you."

Mom hugs me back. She's crying a lot, and I feel bad for bringing up things that are hard for her to talk about. I can tell it's the kind of pain that has been buried deep inside for a long, long time, like an infection that's been slowly spreading into every part of her life—and now it's starting to spread into mine.

Even though it's weird to see Mom as a real person with hurt feelings, who wasn't always an adult and my mom, it helps me to know that her rules about food don't have anything to do with me. And right now, Mom doesn't feel so far away.

Ms. Varna hands Mom a box of tissues.

"Thank you." Mom takes out a few and wipes away her tears.

Dad holds Mom's hand. "We'll take the names of the therapists for Sarah too. It makes sense for us to consider all the options."

Mom doesn't argue.

Ms. Varna opens her notebook and copies down a few names and numbers and hands the paper to Dad.

"What if I can't be what Sarah needs?" Mom asks. "Even if I go to therapy and try everything?"

"That's why we're meeting today," Ms. Varna says. "You don't have to be able to handle this on your own." Her words make me wonder if maybe everyone needs help sometimes. "We're going to come up with a plan to support Sarah that also works for everyone in this room."

"Okay," Mom says. "That sounds really good."

"I'm going to jump in here and offer a practical suggestion. I think we need to transfer the responsibility of food shopping for the family to Dad."

"I'd love that," Dad says. "But it might be hard. I'm out of town a lot for work, and I'm not usually home for dinner. I can't always get to the store."

"You don't have to go to the store all the time," Ms. Varna says. "You can do a big shopping trip once a week or you can order groceries or even have meals delivered. You just need to be the person who makes sure there's always enough food in the house."

"Yes!" Dad says. "I can definitely do that."

"I can help make the list!" I say.

"Wonderful," Ms. Varna says to me, then looks at my parents. "I'd like Sarah to be able to go back to basketball today, but I need your consent to let her play."

Mom looks at me. "When did you stop practicing?"

"I sat out on Tuesday. I was waiting to talk to you about everything at once."

"I understand," Mom says. "You have our permission to practice or do any after-school activities you want."

"Except cooking," I say.

Mom shakes her head. "I should have been more support-ive of that. I'm sorry I wasn't. Cooking has been making you happy, hasn't it?"

"Yeah." I nod.

"Maybe we should see if there's a class you can take. It's good to try new things."

"Thanks," I say, because it's nice to hear that Mom thinks it would be okay if I wanted to become a different ver-sion of me.

After Mom and Dad leave for work, I stay in Ms. Varna's office.

She sighs.

I do too.

"That was hard for me, so I can't begin to imagine how it felt for you."

I know I can get away with not saying too much right

now, because Ms. Varna feels bad for me, but she wants to help, and she can't if I don't tell her the truth. "Do you think my mom can change?" I ask.

"It sounds like she's really going to try. But change can be bumpy and it can take time."

I nod, because I know what Ms. Varna means. I can't make Mom be all the things I need. I have to be patient with her. But now I know what I need, and I'm going to make sure I get it.

Before I leave Ms. Varna's office, she gives me a book, which is basically all about ignoring rules, lists, and other people's opinions about food and learning to trust yourself and eat what tastes good to you. She thinks it might be helpful for me to read and think more about enjoying food, and says that if I want to talk or ask her any questions before our next meeting, we can find time.

At lunch, Ryan is already sitting with Tamar, Sage, and Emilia. I get a sandwich, an apple, and an orange, because all fruit is good. I put the apple in my bag for later and walk over to the table.

"Just make sure your costume is chic," Tamar says to Emilia.

Emilia's eyes narrow. "When am I not chic?"

I sit down next to Ryan.

They all stare at me.

Ryan takes a bite of her sandwich, and it's so quiet at our table I can hear her chew and swallow.

Tamar glances at Sage and says, "Yalla." I'm pretty sure it's Hebrew. But I don't know what the word means.

Sage and Emilia clearly do, because even though they aren't finished eating, they get up and follow Tamar. They want to make it clear I'm not welcome at their table.

Ryan rolls her eyes. "Ignore them."

"I can't," I blurt.

Her shoulders fall. "Sorry."

"I messed up with Emilia, so it's my own fault."

"Okay, fine. But you did nothing to Tamar or Sage. They're just rude."

"They never liked me," I say. "Even before everything with Emilia."

"Well, that's stupid and it's their loss, because, hello . . . you're the best."

I grin. "Thanks."

She smiles back. "How'd it go with your parents?"

I shrug. "You were right about my mom."

"Ugh. No. I didn't want to be."

"I know," I say.

"Maybe she'll change?"

"I hope so. But even if she does, it could take a while. I need to figure out how to trust myself."

"Totally. That's how it is with my brothers. I have to believe my basketball is important no matter what anyone else says, even my parents. It was really hard at first. But I don't know. I guess I'm actually pretty sick of other people's opinions about me mattering more than mine, especially because other people are wrong, like kind of a lot."

I turn her words over in my head. I realize it's not just Mom who's wrong about me. It's Tamar and Sage too, and probably a lot of other people, and I'm not sure why I thought they were more right about me than me.

We eat for a while. I finish half my sandwich and stop. I don't want to be scared to eat more, but I am. I breathe and take one bite out of the second half, and then another. Until I'm finished. And it feels a little less bad than yesterday.

"I almost forgot to tell you!" I say. "I can practice with the team!"

"Yes! That's amazing, especially because all my excuses for why you were sitting out again were really terrible."

"Mine too." I smile. It feels good that Ryan gets what I'm going through and that I'm not the only one who has to figure some things out on my own.

When I walk onto the court for practice, I hear a few girls whispering to one another. I block them out. They don't need to know why I didn't practice on Tuesday or why I'm back now. They're wrong about me, I tell myself. They've been wrong this whole time.

I'm not sure if it's random luck or if Coach Lemon thought about what would be best for me, but we spend most of practice running shooting drills. We work on pressured jump shots and dribble handoffs and fast breaks. I drain almost every shot. I love the way the ball looks and feels when it flies out of my hand through the air and rips the net. Each time I make a basket, my heart skips and dances around. No matter how many times it happens, it never gets old.

We're almost done with practice when Coach Lemon has us circle up. "I want to spend the rest of our time together on rebounding."

"Ugh," someone says.

"Perfect timing," Coach Lemon says back. "No one ever wants to practice rebounding. Everyone wants to stand around the perimeter and shoot threes all game. Rebounding isn't glamorous, but you can score a lot of points on the offensive glass, and it's an opportunity to stand out. If you can get a rebound and have an uncontested layup, it's the best shot in the game. A lot of big-time players have built entire careers on being great at rebounding. You don't have to be a certain size or have a specific skill set. It's all about getting the position and wanting it more than everyone else." Coach Lemon and I don't make eye contact, but I can tell she's talking to me. She wants me to know there's an important job for me on her team.

Our last drill is a two-on-two box-out. We line up, and I end up at the back. On one side, Ryan starts on offense and Ines is on defense, and on the other side, Emilia is on defense and Sage is on offense. Coach Lemon throws the ball toward the rim. Ines and Emilia block out and Ryan and Sage go after the rebound. Ines gets it easily and passes back to Coach Lemon.

The next group goes. Ines gets the offensive rebound and puts it back, but she misses, and the defense gets the board.

When it's finally my turn, I'm on offense against Tamar.

Coach Lemon shoots. Tamar tries to box me out, but I know I want the rebound more. I have to end practice feeling strong. I nudge Tamar underneath the rim, where she can't get to the ball. Before I realize what's happening, I put the ball back up and in for the score!

We run the same drill a few more times until practice is over. I get one other chance on offense, and I score again.

Ryan's mom picks us up after practice and drops me off at my house.

My parents aren't home. There's dinner in the fridge. It's the regular kind with two things—vegetables and cod. Dad also texted me to say he'd go food shopping tomorrow for the week, but if I wanted or needed anything specific for tonight or tomorrow morning to text and he would make it happen.

I'm not ready to eat yet, so I read the first few chapters of the book Ms. Varna gave me. It's about learning to love food and how if you focus on eating what you actually want, you'll end up being happier and even healthier. There's also a lot of information about trusting your body, which sounds like it should be easy but is really hard, because of this thing called diet culture that we're all part of without even knowing it exists, which is totally unfair. I don't want to be part of it anymore. There's even a section on bad information. I never thought about it before, but you really do have to be careful and pick reliable sources and people to trust, because even if your friends and family mean well, they can still be wrong about what's healthy for you.

The book also makes me realize how often people say "healthy" when they mean "skinny," which is so wrong, because you can be healthy and also unhealthy at any size. Like Mom. And me, until now.

I take a break from reading and make a plate of food. Then I turn on a few more lights, because the kitchen is making me sad. I don't get how we had this great meeting with Ms. Varna and here I am eating by myself again. I'm about to warm up my dinner when I hear the garage door open and Mom's shoes click-clacking against the floor, which is weird, because we're a no-shoe house. When I look up, she's standing in front of me with her coat still on, holding a big bag. "I'm sorry, honey. I didn't want you to eat alone, but I went to pick up a few things and they didn't have what I wanted at the first store, so I made a second stop, but there was so much traffic." She closes her eyes and shakes her head. "It's so stupid. I have a PhD, but I didn't know where to buy Doritos."

"You bought me Doritos?" My words barely make it out.

"Please tell me you like Spicy Nacho. Those are the ones, right?"

I nod, and before I realize it, I'm crying and so is Mom, and we're hugging.

I hold on as tight as I can, because I feel loved and safe and seen in a way I don't think I've ever felt before, and I never want this to end.

Mom puts everything she bought out on the table with the dinner she made, and we sit together, just the two of us, and eat. I try a few of the different sides she picked up on her way home. There's baba ghanoush, grape leaves stuffed with rice, and a chickpea salad. We eat and talk and trade books back and forth.

It feels good to be full. But weird in my brain. I'm scared to change. I don't want my body to feel like it's not mine again. And I'm afraid I won't ever really be able to accept myself or feel happy being me. But the food tastes good, so I put more on my plate. It feels like I'm playing Whac-A-Mole in my head, blocking out the rules and lists and voices. And even though it's weird to ignore everything I thought was true and important about food, as soon as I start, I can tell it's going to get easier.

When I'm done, I go upstairs to my room and start my homework, and after a while, I want something salty and bad for me. Wait, no—not bad. Just salty and also crunchy.

That's when I remember there are Doritos in the kitchen!

I go downstairs, take the chips from the cabinet, and pop open the bag. The smell of fake cheese is strong and familiar. *All foods are good.* I put a chip in my mouth. It tastes even better than I remember. Then I eat another one. And another. Then a few more. They're exactly what I wanted.

After I finish my homework, I make a grocery list for Dad. I add pretzels and peanuts and crackers and bananas to the top, because I want to have other snacks too. I leave the list on Dad's desk where I know he'll see it.

THIRTEEN

THE NEXT DAY, I keep waiting to feel big and bloated, especially after I add a peach to my yogurt at breakfast, but when I'm finished eating, I feel fine. Better than fine. All morning, I actually forget to think about food or what I ate or didn't eat or want to eat.

Ryan and I have lunch together by ourselves in the back of the cafeteria. I got pizza, because it smelled so good and it was exactly what I wanted. The warm red sauce, melty cheese, and crispy crust taste even better than I imagined. I'm halfway through my slice when Ryan says, "I have to tell you something."

I look up at her, and as soon as I do, I know that whatever

she's about to say is bad, because she keeps biting her finger-nails and she hasn't touched her food. "What?"

"Tamar is having a Chef Junior–themed party next Friday before the auditions. It's a boy-girl thing. I RSVPed yes before I knew you weren't invited."

"Wait, so you're going?" My throat feels swollen.

"I don't have a choice. I'm Emilia's partner for the milkshake-making contest. I can't ditch her," she says. It's hard to breathe. "Are you okay? Are you mad at me?"

I don't know what I am or how I feel and I don't want to lie to her. "When did Tamar send out the invites?"

"Last Friday."

"Seriously?"

"I was going to tell you after the dance, but then all that stuff happened with Benny and Emilia and you fell at the game, and I just kept forgetting about the party, because it didn't matter compared to everything else."

"So, did she text everyone before school or something?" I ask. I have this sinking feeling in my stomach that I was never on the list in the first place. I know it shouldn't matter, but it feels important. It's proof that I was right this whole time about how Tamar and Sage were just waiting to get rid of me.

"No. After school," Ryan says. "I bet she took you off the list when she found out about you and Benny being partners."

"Yeah. Maybe."

"I'm sorry. It stinks. And the party is going to be way less fun without you."

"Then don't go." My words taste desperate.

Ryan looks at her food and pulls on the end of her ponytail, like she's thinking about what to say, and I don't get why it's taking her so long to tell me she's not going anymore. She's my best friend. She's supposed to have my back no matter what and pick me over Tamar and Sage and Emilia and their stupid party. "I'd feel weird if I didn't go, when I said I would."

It stings behind my eyes, and I'm afraid if I say anything else, I'll cry.

If everything were different and Emilia were still my BFF, she'd never go without me. She'd boycott or make Tamar invite me. "Please don't go." My voice cracks. "It feels like you're picking them over me."

"It's not about you!" Ryan says. "I don't want there to be sides. I want to be able to go to the party and have that be okay and have you still be my best friend. I mean, it's not cool that Tamar did this, but if the Chef Junior thing hadn't happened I'd obviously call her out and force her to invite you."

"You would?"

"Duh!" she says. "But Emilia is still hurt."

"Yeah. I mean, I get that. Why didn't you just say that before?"

"I shouldn't have to! We're BFFs. I can't only hang out with the people you like. That's not fair." She pauses. "You're asking me to tiptoe around you because you feel bad about yourself. And I really don't get that either—I mean, you're fun and pretty and smart and good at basketball and apparently cooking too."

I bite down on the inside of my mouth and try to push my tears back, but they trickle down my face. "I'm afraid I'm never going to see that person. It feels like there are confident people and non-confident people and we're stuck like ice cubes in our little sections."

"No way," Ryan says. "Maybe you have to risk getting your hopes up and being let down. But you're not stuck. You can turn into one of those confident people."

Ryan makes it sound possible. "I really want to," I say.

I already know I'm going to feel bad tomorrow, when

Ryan is at the party without me. There's no instant fix for the hole deep inside me, the one I've been trying to ignore by spending so much time thinking about food. But it helps to say it's there, twisting up the way I see myself and messing with my view of everything. It makes me think the more I say I'm not okay and I'm seeing things wrong, the better I'll actually be.

After school, Mom drives me to Benny's house, because we only have a week left before Chef Junior auditions. On the ride, Mom and I try to figure out why we like British detective stories the best. And it feels a little easier to sit next to each other since we talked about everything with Ms. Varna. The air between us doesn't feel so thick and cloudy the way it did before.

Benny and I are in his kitchen with the timer counting down from twenty minutes, because that's how long we'll have to make our dish in the competition. I'm peeling and chopping garlic cloves for sumac fish and rice when Benny asks, "What are you dressing up as for Tamar's?"

"It's a costume party?" I ask.

"Uh. Yeah. You have to dress up as a food. I'm going as pizza," he says. "You know you need a costume or she won't let you in. She's intense about that kind of thing."

"She won't let me in anyway. I'm not invited."

He looks confused. "I thought everyone in the grade was invited."

I bite down on my lip. "Not me. But it's my fault. I was a bad friend to Emilia." I put the garlic in the food processor with the walnuts, parsley, and mint.

Benny finishes coating the fish, slides the pan in the oven to broil, and then sets the timer. "What did you do?"

My stomach dips. "I can't say. I don't want things to get weird or whatever."

"They won't," he says. "Just tell me."

I take a deep breath. I can't actually believe I'm about to say this out loud, because this totally seems like something a confident person would do, but then I say it. "I like you." My cheeks get hot. "I lied to Emilia about Chef Junior, because I didn't want her to find out about my, um, crush, so she's allowed to be mad at me basically forever if she wants." I keep my eyes trained on the food in front of me; I can't look at him right now.

"Oh." He sounds surprised. "I, uh, like you too." His voice is so soft that I'm not sure I heard him right, but I can't ask him to say it again. I risk looking up, and he's smiling at me, like he really does like me, and I can't help but smile back.

My heart is pounding. "I can't go out with you." The words are in the air before I can stop myself, but I know it's true. I can't. It doesn't matter that I really want to be BF-GF with Benny. I need to get strong on my own without a boyfriend. No one else can change how I feel about myself. Not Ryan or Benny or anyone. That's up to me.

"Yeah, me neither. I mean, I can't, like, handle a girlfriend right now, not with everything that's going on with my family," he says. "But I still wish you were coming to Tamar's party."

"Me too," I say.

The fish and rice cook, until the whole room starts to smell like turmeric. Once our dish is done cooling off, I try a few bites. It's perfect—browned and delicious.

Before Mom picks me up, I ask Benny if I can take what we made home for Mom, Dad, and me to have for dinner or maybe lunch tomorrow, in case there's nothing else to eat. He makes a plate for himself and then wraps up the rest for me.

It turns out Dad came home early and made baked chicken, roasted asparagus, and mashed potatoes, but it feels good to have an extra meal in our fridge, especially one that I put there.

After we eat as a family, Dad doesn't have to go back into his office to do work, so we change and head outside to shoot hoops and practice rebounding. He shows me a few different ways to box out, because rebounding was actually Dad's thing in college, when he wasn't the tallest or fastest anymore, when he had to practice other skills to prove himself and elevate the team. Same as me.

I already liked the idea of being great at rebounding, but now that I know it was Dad's thing too, it feels like something else we have in common.

Dad shows me how to rebound on offense, which Coach Lemon didn't really get into that much. It's weird how sometimes you can feel like the least important player on the court, but actually you're the most important. For example, if you're in the corner and not part of the set play, you might feel left out, but you can still help spread the defense to make space for your teammates or get an open shot or an offensive rebound.

When we're done shooting hoops, Dad and I walk into the garage.

He's about to open the door to the house when he stops and looks at me. "I should have taken charge of food shopping a long time ago. I'm sorry."

"Why didn't you?" I ask.

He clears his throat. "I knew what I was getting into when I married Mom. Food has always been hard for her. I think it's what she told you, but also her family was controlling. This was one way she could be in charge of herself. I didn't think about how her problems might affect you. And I guess the way I was raised, I didn't really think about men feeding families, which is unfair. I'm your parent. I'm responsible for making sure there's food for you."

"But what if Mom says there's too much food? Are you sure you won't take her side?"

"Why would you think that?" he asks.

"Because I heard you talking. You were worried about me, and Mom convinced you not to be."

"Oh, Sarah. I'm sorry you had to hear that. And I'm sorry I didn't stand up for you." Dad sighs. "You're right. I had a feeling something was wrong, but I didn't want it to be. I know how big Mom's issues are—I couldn't imagine seeing anything like that in you. I didn't realize the problem would be there whether we talked about it or not. It's different now. I'm going to help you."

Dad opens his arms, and I sink into him. And even though I know I need to learn to trust myself, it feels good that Dad is going to be here for me.

FOURTEEN

ON MONDAY MORNING, I meet with Ms. Varna. I like that we get to check in early. It helps to have a reminder first thing that I can be kind to myself.

"I haven't been thinking about food as much as before," I say. "But that feeling is still there all the time, like maybe it would be easier to be me if I ate less. Will that ever go away?"

Ms. Varna puts down her pencil. "You know how before you talked to Coach Lemon, the feeling was so big and taking over every thought and everything you did? And since that moment, it's been getting smaller, and you've had more space for other thoughts besides food?"

"Yeah," I say.

"It's going to keep getting smaller as you practice changing your thought patterns around food. Until you're in charge of how and when you think about eating. You're building trust with yourself that you'll be okay, even if you let go of your fears and allow your relationship with food to change."

"So it's going to keep changing until it's something else?"

"Exactly," she says. "It will take time and some days will be hard, but you can recover from disordered eating."

I can't imagine what that will be like, but I trust Ms. Varna. "Do you think I could come in another day too? Just until I start seeing a therapist outside school."

"Of course. I'm happy you asked." Ms. Varna opens her notebook and looks at her calendar. "How about Wednesdays at break?"

"That's perfect," I say. "Thank you."

"You should be proud of yourself, Sarah."

"I am," I say, because I know what I'm doing is hard. But I don't want to spend all my time thinking about food and how if I eat or don't eat certain things, I'll feel like I'm in control and okay, when I'm not. I can't be on this roller coaster for the rest of my life. I don't want to end up like Mom. I feel bad as soon as the thought comes into my mind, but I know it's true. I deserve more.

The rest of the week feels like it goes on forever. Everyone is talking nonstop about Tamar's Chef Junior party. It turns out Benny was right—the entire grade was invited, except me. I try to block out the chatter about costumes and carpools. But it hurts to be left out. It helps that on Wednesday I talk to Ms. Varna about everything I'm feeling, and then after school I cook with Benny one last time before auditions.

On Thursday at lunch, Ryan sits with me in the back of the cafeteria again. "What are you dressing up as for Tamar's?" I ask.

She shakes her head. "I should have said no to the group costume. I mean, I did, but then Tamar was all like, 'That's so not nice. Are you not my friend or something?' It was the worst. She wouldn't let the group costume go. We're going as hors d'oeuvres. I'm shrimp cocktail. Emilia is bacon-wrapped scallops. Tamar is cheese. And Sage is crackers." She rolls her eyes. "It's so dumb."

"It's cute," I say. Even though I wish it didn't feel like Ryan was in a group with girls who don't like me, I remind myself we're best friends. Not them.

"All I'm saying is you as Spicy Nacho and me as Cool Ranch Doritos would have been a way better costume."

"Duh." I smile. "That's actually perfect."

We both eat for a few minutes.

"I'm nervous for auditions," I say. "I mean, at first I wanted to hang out with Benny and learn how to cook, but now I really like cooking and I want to make Chef Junior."

"You will. Just believe you can."

"But I don't want to jinx myself."

"That's not a real thing. It's just a stupid way to not feel bad if you lose," Ryan says. "Maybe try knowing you deserve a spot, because, I mean, you do."

I turn her words over. "I've never done that before," I say, because I realize I've always been afraid, even in basketball. It's weird to think about trying something else. But I have to stop being scared, if I'm going to learn to trust myself—if I'm ever going to be confident.

"If it doesn't work, you can always go back to being afraid," Ryan says.

I laugh.

She does too.

"I think it's so cool that you learned how to cook and now you're a legit chef. I want to try something I've never done before too—that I don't have to share with my brothers."

"I can teach you how to cook."

"Baked mac and cheese?" she asks.

"Sure! Well, I've actually never made that, but I can totally figure it out."

"Let's do it together after you win Chef Junior," Ryan says.

"Yes! We can celebrate my victory with more cooking!" I say.

I'm excited about having things be different. It makes me feel like I can win, like it's possible. Like anything is.

After school, I change for our game, lace up my basketball sneakers, walk onto the court and over to Coach Lemon. "I've been practicing rebounding a lot," I say.

"That's great, Sarah."

"And thanks for helping me, um, come up with a plan. I think it's going to make things better at home. It already is."

"I'm really happy to hear that." She grins.

I smile and jog over to join the layup line.

I don't start, but Coach Lemon puts me in early and keeps me in for most of the game. She only takes me out for a few minutes at the end of the third quarter and then puts me back in halfway through the fourth quarter, when we're tied.

We're almost out of time when a girl on the other team

puts up a shot. I step between the hoop and the girl I'm guarding, stick my butt out into her waist, and push her back, the perfect box out, like Dad taught me. The ball comes off the rim, and I pull the rebound. I turn and make an outlet pass to Tamar. She makes it to half court before the whistle blows because Coach Lemon has called a time-out.

We huddle around her, and she draws up the play—a staggered double ball screen to get Ryan a layup.

I'm not one of the players setting the screen. I'm in the corner. It makes me feel like I'm not good enough to be front and center and in the middle of the action. *Stop. That's not real.* I've played almost the entire game. I take a deep breath. That's when I realize Coach Lemon put me in the corner because it's the best position to get an open three if Ryan drives and dishes, or to crash the boards if she pulls up for a jumper. Coach Lemon is counting on me to be there and make a play if I get a chance, and I know I can.

When the whistle blows again, I stay on the sideline to inbound the ball. I pass to Ryan, then sprint to the corner. It doesn't matter that I'm a little slower. I still get there in time, just as Ryan is starting to go around the screens.

Only the other team is defending the play perfectly, switching the screens, so Ryan can't get to the hoop for a layup, and no one is open. She doesn't have a choice but to take an outside shot.

As soon as the ball is in the air, I know it's going long. I run toward the hoop, but my defender is still between me and the basket. It helps that I'm bigger and taller than her, because I can use my size to dominate and move her toward the hoop, where I have the best angle to get the ball. It feels good to take up space.

When the ball comes off the left side of the rim, I jump and tap it off the backboard and into the hoop.

Err. The horn sounds.

I did it! I made the winning basket! We won!

Ryan runs over to me, shouting, "Buzzer beater!" She's shrieking and hugging me and jumping up and down. We high-five, low-five, pivot-turn, and fist-bump.

Nothing is like it used to be anymore. But I can feel myself getting stronger and I know where to be and what I can do to help my team and myself in small ways that add up to big things.

On Friday night, Dad is home from his work trip and dinner is spaghetti with meat sauce, salad, and a baguette. I fill my plate up with everything, and so does Dad.

Mom takes mostly salad and a little pasta. She doesn't take any bread.

I can't stop thinking about the auditions tomorrow. The nerves hit me in waves. It's been like this all day. One minute, I'm ready to compete and confident I can cook really well. Benny and I are a great team. I can do this. Then out of nowhere, fear crashes into me so hard it knocks me off balance. I'm going to mess up, and we won't get picked. I don't matter. *No. Stop. Breathe.* I'm worth believing in.

We eat for a few minutes, and then Mom moves the basket of sliced baguette to the other side of the table, like she's afraid of what will happen if it's too close to her or if she accidentally eats a piece or two.

Dad doesn't say anything to Mom and neither do I.

Mom and I tell Dad about my game yesterday and how awesome I played.

I don't let myself think about what it means that Mom moved the bread or what she's trying to tell me. *Mom is wrong about food.* I pick up the piece of baguette on my plate, dip it into the sauce, and take a small bite. It tastes warm and salty and tomato-y. *All food is good*, I tell myself until I'm done with my bread and the food on my plate.

After dinner, I start to get nervous again. My hands are

shaky, which is really not going to work. I have to be steady when I'm cooking tomorrow. I take a shower and try to calm down.

When I go back to the kitchen to get a snack, Mom is sitting at the table guarding the fridge and reading. She has both hands around a cup of steaming tea, like she's trying to keep warm. I don't ask her for permission to enter. I open the door and look inside.

The shelves and drawers and even the side compartments are packed with food. Dad went shopping again. It smells good, like oranges and honey.

I never want to turn away. I'm afraid if I do, it will all disappear, and I don't want how I feel right now to end.

Dad walks into the kitchen and grabs an apple from the counter. "I got everything on your list, except grapes. They didn't look good. I bought extra blueberries instead."

"Thanks," I say.

"You're welcome. Celtics are on."

"I'll join you in"—Mom glances at her watch—"twenty for the tip. I can't stand the pregame show."

"So boring," I agree.

"Suit yourself." Dad grins and goes back into the family room to watch. And I go back to looking inside our fridge.

"I know it's a lot of food." I can hear panic in Mom's voice. She's overwhelmed. It's too much for her. I feel bad that the thing I need is the exact opposite of what makes her feel safe.

"I'm okay. Thanks. This is good for me." Because I want her to know.

"Oh. Good. I'm so glad," she says, relieved.

I'm in the mood for something sweet, so I take out blueberries and raspberries, and then open the freezer. There's a half-empty bag of semisweet chocolate chips in the door. I make a bowl of fruit and chocolate mixed together. And then I sit down at the table next to Mom and start eating.

"What do you think of Famous Fictional Detectives of the Twentieth and Twenty-First Centuries?" Mom asks.

"OMG!" I shriek. "You got the class!"

"Yes!" She smiles. "I don't think I've ever been this excited to teach anything. Want to help me make a list of detectives?"

"Um, obviously!"

Mom picks up her pen and gets ready to write down my ideas.

"Sherlock, Morse, Marple, Poirot," I say, and then stop myself. "Maybe you should have part of the class be about younger detectives. That way you could include Petra and Calder from *Chasing Vermeer*, the kids from *Mysterious Benedict Society*, and Nik and Norva from *High-Rise*."

"That's such a great idea," Mom says.

"Thanks!"

"I'll go to the library and look at all the books we've read together. There are a lot of good ones."

"Yeah," I say. "There really are." I finish my berries and chocolate and then walk over to the cabinet. I open the Doritos Mom bought me and pour chips into a new bowl.

"Sarah. Really? You're still hungry?" Mom covers her mouth with both hands, like she's trying to catch the words, but they're already out, hanging there in the air between us.

My cheeks get hot, like I'm sitting too close to a fire. I want to scream at her, because I'm doing everything right. I can feel how right I am pulsing through me. I take a deep breath, sit down again, and eat a chip. The cheesy flavor takes over my mouth with the perfect hint of spice.

"I'm sorry," Mom says. "I have a problem with food. And I wish I could help you while you're struggling. But I think the best I can do is not comment on food at all."

"Or make a face," I say.

Mom nods. "I won't do that anymore either."

"Okay. Good," I say, and then I eat a few more chips.

Mom looks at me. "You're so strong."

"Thanks," I say, because I know that's true. But I still wish I didn't have to be. "You're going to talk to someone, right?"

"Next week," Mom says. "A family therapist. She's in the same practice as the specialist Dad scheduled for you, so she can give me parenting strategies. And we're going to work on me too. I'm not sure it's going to change anything—"

"I know," I say. "But I hope it does."

"Me too," she says.

I'm trying so hard to fix the things about me that feel broken, and it feels good that Mom is going to try too.

I finish the chips in my bowl, and just as I'm about to get up to go watch the game, Mom asks, "Why didn't you go to Ryan's tonight?" Like it just occurred to her that it's Friday and I shouldn't be here.

"She's not there. She went to a party at Tamar's. I wasn't invited."

"Why not?" Mom sounds mad for me. "What's happening?"

I shrug. "Everyone was invited, except me." I can feel the tears building up behind my eyes. I drop my head and push them back. "I lied to Emilia about being partners with Benny for Chef Junior. But Tamar and Sage never liked me, even before, and I don't know what I ever did to them."

"Probably nothing," Mom says.

"It feels like there's something wrong with me, and they know."

"Oh, honey, there isn't. You're amazing. I don't know why they can't see that you're a good friend. But you are. Ryan sees it."

"Not enough to not go to the party."

Mom rubs my shoulder. "That doesn't mean she likes them more. She's human, and she likes herself the most. We all do."

"Yeah." I nod. "I get what you mean."

"Do you like Tamar and Sage? Do you want to be friends with them?"

"I don't know. Not really. But they're on the team, and Ryan likes them. And I just wish they didn't not like me."

Mom pulls me in a little closer. "The thing is, no matter what you do, you won't be able to change how they feel about you or how they treat you. You can't change other people, ever." I know that's true. I can't change Mom or fix her problems with food, and I'd do anything to make that happen. "The best you can do is treat them how you want them to treat you, stand up for yourself, and then don't waste your energy worrying what they think. I know that's especially hard right now when you can't avoid them, but it's good practice. There will be Tamars and Sages for the rest of your life."

"I thought things were supposed to get better when you're older."

She smiles. "Some things do. Most things. But not everything. There are always parties you're not invited to and people who hurt your feelings. They just don't matter as much, because you can make different friends who appreciate you."

"That sounds impossible."

"I know, honey, but trust me, it's possible."

I wish it could always be like this with Mom.

I watch part of the Celtics game with my parents, but at the end of the first quarter, I get nervous about Chef Junior again. I really want to make it onto the show.

The one good part about not being invited to Tamar's party is that I can go to bed early. Meanwhile everyone else from our school who's competing tomorrow will probably be tired from staying up late and standing around or whatever you do at a boy-girl party.

After I brush my teeth and get into bed, my phone buzzes. It's a text from Ryan: **I'm so bored. This party is awkward + trying too hard + my costume is really itchy.**

Weird, I write back. **And UGH!**

My mom is picking me up soon, because of the boredom. We might give Benny a ride home too. He's freaking out about tomorrow.

I try on confidence to see how it feels, like it's a headband or a bracelet, something easy to slide on and off. **Did you tell him we're definitely going to make it onto the show?!**

Obvs!!!

Thanks ☺. You're the best.

☺ ☺ ☺.

FIFTEEN

THE NEXT DAY, my stomach starts growling on the ride to school, even though I finished breakfast right before I got in the car. I grab the banana from my bag, peel it, and take a bite and then another. It tastes good and my stomach starts to settle down. I eat until it's gone. I'm not sure if Mom murmurs or makes a comment. I'm not paying attention. I'm too busy listening to what I need.

Mom pulls into the drop-off line, like it's a regular school day. She stops the car and then turns to me. "How are you feeling about the audition?"

"Ready," I say, because I'm trying as hard as I can to be

confident. "Benny and I are really good. We'll get on the show. I know it."

Mom grins. "You've got this! Dad and I will be back in a few hours to pick you up and celebrate."

"Thanks." I smile back.

I walk into school, and the hall by the cafeteria is packed with competitors and their families. My permission forms were already sent in, so I didn't need a parent to come with me. There are signs pointing to the room where auditions are being livestreamed for families. I didn't realize that parents would be able to stay and watch. It makes me wish Mom were still here to cheer me on.

I turn around to check the parking lot, but she's gone. And I guess I know Mom won't want to be around food all day. So, I take out my phone and text Dad. He told me to tell him if I ever needed him, and I do. **Could you please come to school and watch me audition?**

Dad texts back right away: **Of course! I'll head over now.**

Thank you!

I'm really glad you asked.

Me too! It makes me realize we all need different things, even if we're in the same family. I can't just expect other people to know what I want unless I tell them, and sometimes even my parents need extra help to hear me.

When I look up from my phone, Tamar and Sage are huddled together a few feet away, taking selfies with closed smiles. They're made-up and camera-ready.

I hear Sage giggle when I walk by. I stop and turn around to face her and Tamar. "Good luck," I say. I get that they don't like me that much, but I know Chef Junior matters to them, and I hope they do their best in the audition.

"Yeah. Uh," Tamar stutters. "I mean, thanks. You too."

"Thanks," I say back.

Then Sage whispers something in Tamar's ear, and they both start laughing. But I walk away, because I don't even know for sure that they're laughing at me, and right now, I don't care what they think. There's nothing I can do about it anyway. Plus, I'm glad I was nice, even if they weren't.

As soon as I see Benny standing at the end of the hall, my heart starts pounding. I remind myself to breathe. I have to wait in line and hand my phone over to someone from the show, so it takes me a few minutes to get over to Benny, but when I finally do, I see Ryan standing next to him.

"Surprise," Benny and Ryan both say at the same time.

"What are you doing here?" I ask Ryan. "Wait, are you

competing against us?" Because I'm pretty sure only competitors and their families are allowed to be in this area right now.

"Um, no. You know I don't cook. I asked Duke if he could get me special permission to watch, and he did! So, I'm your team cheerleader. Ready to celebrate your victory."

"OMG! Best surprise ever!" I shriek, and wrap my arms around her.

She hugs me back. "It was all Benny's idea. I just thought it was a good one."

I look at Benny. "Thanks."

"You're welcome." He smiles at me. My stomach flips. "Also, you should know, we're in group one."

"Eek!" I say. "But also good! I'd much rather go first than wait around and get even more freaked out than I already am."

"Ditto." Benny puts up his hand, and I high-five him.

That's when I notice his eyes are red and swollen, and he looks tired or something else. "Are you okay?" I ask.

"I'm great." He grins. "Ready to cook."

There's a loud screeching noise, and then someone starts talking into a microphone. "I'd like to invite all registered teams to make their way into the cafeteria. Parents, please head to the classrooms at the end of the hall. You'll be able to watch your chefs compete on the livestream from there. Thank you in advance for your cooperation. Good luck, chefs!"

The doors to the cafeteria open, and everyone who's competing rushes inside. I can feel how nervous I am, and how badly I want to make it onto the show.

Ryan grabs my hand and squeezes. "You're going to get picked."

"I know." I squeeze back. "Thanks for coming," I say, because even though I know I can do this, it helps to have my best friend here to believe in me too.

My heart is racing as Benny and I walk in together. The cafeteria doesn't look anything like it did yesterday. There are cameras and lights and a studio set that makes me feel someplace far away from school and real life.

I recognize Emily Ying—the host of Chef Junior—right away. She's standing in the front of the room holding a microphone. Her grandmothers taught her how to cook together, and now she's famous for her Chinese-Jewish fusion, which I think is so cool. Her brisket dumplings and potato scallion pancakes are in the freezer section of practically every grocery store.

I stand a little closer to Benny than I normally would if

it were a regular school day. He smells good, like soap and spearmint gum. I tie my hair back into a low ponytail, and when I'm done, my arm brushes up against his. He doesn't move away, and I don't either. We stand there in the middle of the crowded cafeteria, listening to the rules, with our arms pressed together. It feels good to be this close to him and to know that for right now we both feel the same way about each other. I never want this to end.

"This is your chance to show off your culinary skills for our judges." Emily gestures to the three chefs sitting behind a large rectangular table. I also recognize them from the show. "And we want you to have fun cooking!

"When your group number is called, please find your station. Then we'll unveil the four main ingredients you'll be using along with items from the basic pantry. You'll have five minutes to brainstorm with your teammate and twenty minutes to make your dish. After you're finished, you'll go back to the classrooms while the judges taste and deliberate.

"There are four rounds of ten pairs auditioning today. Once all the groups have gone, we'll pick two teams from each group to compete next weekend live on our YouTube channel! What do you think? Are you ready?"

We all start cheering and clapping. And I can't stop smiling. Because I'm excited!

"Amazing! Let's get started!" Emily says. "Group one, please be at your station in ten minutes."

Everyone who isn't in the first group leaves the cafeteria.

Benny and I walk over to the set and find our station. We cover our hair, put on aprons, wash our hands, and look around to see what we have—an oven, four burners, a sink, cutting boards, knives, bowls, and every kind of utensil imaginable. I don't recognize most of the kids who are competing against us, which means they must be from different middle schools. But I know it doesn't matter. This isn't basketball. I can't tell anything about their cooking from looking around the room or watching what they do to prepare, and I don't have to change anything I'm doing for them.

When I turn back to Benny, he's leaning against the counter, staring at the floor, like he's about to puke.

"Are you okay?" I take a few steps closer to him.

He shakes his head.

"Nervous? Or sick?"

He shuts his eyes. And before I can think about what I'm doing or who's watching me, I hold his hand. It's warm and clammy, which I don't expect, like he's burning up. "You're the best cook I know," I say. "And we're a really good team. We can do this."

He squeezes my hand. "I know. I'm not nervous," he says. "I lied before about being great. On the way here, my mom told me that Asha has to stay longer. She wants to. She's not ready to come home."

"I'm sorry," I say. I know how much he misses his sister. "Do you know when she'll be ready?"

He shrugs. "They didn't say. I guess she doesn't know."

I'm pretty sure I can say something to help Benny, so I swallow and decide to be confident. "It's not the same thing, but I've been having some, um, problems with disordered eating, and before, I really didn't want help. But now I do, and I'm doing everything I can to change how I eat and feel about food. It sounds like Asha is really trying to change too."

"I'm glad you're getting help now," he says. "Asha's doctors always say the earlier you start, the better."

"Really? I didn't know that."

He nods. "She's been acting so different. I guess I assumed staying was bad, because anything different has been bad for so long, but maybe you're right and this time different is actually good. I mean, she knows she's not ready, and she wants to be."

"I really hope so," I say.

"Thanks. Me too."

"We don't have to compete, if you're not up for it. We can walk out right now."

Benny thinks about my offer for a minute. "I really want to cook."

"Okay. Good." I want that too.

"Welcome to Chef Junior," Chef Emily says into the microphone. "Your four ingredients today are salmon, dates, rice, and chickpeas. When you hear the buzzer, your twenty-minute cooking time will automatically start, so get right to work."

Benny and I don't need five minutes to figure out what we're making. We have most of what we need for a version of his mom's chickpea and date tagine. We just don't have enough time to make the actual recipe, because that takes at least two hours, so we spend our five minutes coming up with a quick version of the dish. I'm in charge of the salmon, and Benny is handling the improvised tagine.

When the buzzer sounds, I rinse and pat and season, then I add olive oil to the pan and turn on the burner. I check to make sure the pan is hot, but not too hot, before I put the fish in skin-side down. I set the timer and watch the oil bubble around the edges. Only when the timer beeps, I wait. The fish doesn't look ready to be flipped yet and I know I need to follow my instincts. I'm so focused I almost forget about the clock and the competition and the cameras.

I flip each piece, and as soon as I do, I'm so glad I waited. I can tell by the way it feels on my spatula that it's perfect. I set the timer again. When the salmon is done, I carefully transfer each piece onto the plates with the rice.

We have four minutes left.

I walk over to help Benny with the garnish, but as soon as I'm next to him, I can tell something is wrong. I sniff again to be sure. "That smell."

"What?" he asks, without looking up.

"That's not parsley. It's cilantro."

Benny stops chopping. He looks panicked. "You're right. How did I not notice?"

We don't have time to talk. I sprint across the kitchen, grab parsley, sprint back, rinse, and hand it to Benny, because we only have two minutes.

He doesn't stop to measure or look at the clock. He chops, mixes, tastes, adds the garnish to each plate, and then we hear *errrrr* as the buzzer sounds.

Benny and I don't say anything while we walk down the

hall. I keep thinking about how the judges are in there right now tasting our dish. I'm proud of what we made. I know it was good. If we don't win, it's not because of something we did wrong. Not everyone is always going to agree or like the same things. Like with Tamar and Sage and how I'm just not their favorite, and there's nothing I can do about it. It doesn't mean I'm not great or that I should change and try to be different.

"I really think we're going to get picked," I say to Benny.

"Me too," he says.

"Thanks for, you know, teaching me how to cook. I'm really into it. It's like my favorite thing to do now."

He smiles at me. "No problem."

"Now I just need to find a way to keep cooking after this is all over."

"There's actually this, um, sauces class that I want to take. It's free at the community center, so you just have to sign up and bring your own apron. Would you maybe want to take it too? Like with me?"

"Yes!" I say. "I mean, I have to ask my parents, but they'll say yes. My mom already said I could take a cooking class if I wanted."

"Awesome." Benny takes a deep breath, relieved.

Benny stops in the bathroom, and I head down the hall to find Ryan.

She's waiting in one of the classrooms with Dad—and Mom!

Mom rushes over and hugs me. "You are amazing, honey! You really are!"

"Thank you," I say, because I know that's true. I feel amazing.

"You should be so proud of yourself," Dad says.

"I am." I hug him too.

"I'm glad you asked us to be here." Mom is beaming. "It was really incredible to see you in action. You're so good."

I smile wide, because I can tell she really means it. "Thanks for watching!"

"I don't know if this matters," Ryan says, "but yours was one hundred percent the prettiest. It looked seriously profesh."

"Oh, it matters," I say. "Everything does."

"It wasn't even close," Dad says.

Mom is nodding too, like she agrees.

I don't even care that Ryan, Mom, and Dad are obviously biased. I feel like I already won.

Right before the last round starts, I get up and go out into the hall. I'm too excited to sit and wait in silence for another twenty-five minutes.

Emilia is standing at the other end of the empty hallway. I wonder if her parents changed their minds about letting her compete or if Duke got her in too.

We haven't talked since our pickup game, since she said she didn't want to be friends anymore. I keep walking until I'm standing in front of her.

She looks up at me, and I wait a few seconds, thinking maybe she's about to pretend I'm not there and walk away, but she doesn't.

"I'm sorry I lied," I say. "I should have talked to you about being partners with Benny for Chef Junior before I said yes. And I don't expect you to forgive me or to want to be friends again, but I get how badly I messed up, and I'm really sorry."

Emilia shifts on her feet. "It's okay. I mean, I wish you'd trusted me not to be mad, but also, I get why you didn't. So, apology accepted," she says. "I'm sorry too. It wasn't fair for me to shut you out like that. And I wish I could take back that stuff I said about you not eating. It was mean. My parents are sort of controlling about, like, everything. That's why I'm not allowed to have friends over. They think kids are messy, even though we're not, like, little anymore, and we don't have sticky fingers or whatever. I guess I just wanted friends to be easy, but that's not actually reasonable. I should have told you."

"Thanks for telling me now," I say.

"It's not a secret or anything, but it's sort of embarrassing."

"I won't tell."

"Cool," she says. "Thanks."

I nod. "Oh, and, um, you were right. I've been having issues with food." It stings behind my eyes. I can feel the tears coming, and then everything looks blurry.

"I'm sorry." She bites her lip. "I didn't know you had a real problem. I would never have acted like that if I—I just thought you wanted attention."

"I mean, technically it's not a disorder. But there are a lot of other people like me, who are having a hard time and have symptoms, but can't be diagnosed."

"That must be hard to, like, know you have a problem, but then you're like—wait, but do I? And you need help, but you don't feel like you should get it."

"Yeah." I nod. "That's exactly how it feels."

"That's so not fair," she says.

"Thanks," I say. Emilia always makes everything I'm thinking feel more true.

"For the record, if you still like Benny, he's all yours. I like someone else now. I'm not saying who, but he's in the same friend group, and really cute, and we have way more in common. Benny and I had nothing to talk about, since, no offense, but I hate cooking and reading and that's, like, all he likes."

We both laugh.

"I still like him," I say. "But I don't want a boyfriend right now."

"Oh. That's cool. It's actually like way cooler to have a crush on someone and not want a boyfriend than to be all like, OMG, I need to be BF/GF. But if you do change your mind, it's totally fine with me."

"Good to know," I say. "I miss talking to you."

"Me too," she says back. "Let's hang soon."

"Definitely." It feels good that Emilia and I could maybe be friends again in a new way that makes more sense for us.

"OMG! We bombed," Tamar says, walking over with Sage.

"But on the plus side, we looked super cute." Sage twirls her hair.

Tamar shakes her head. "It was humiliating."

Sage glances at me, like she's just noticing I'm here now, and then she looks back at Emilia. "Everything okay?"

"Yeah. Sarah and I are good," Emilia says. "There's no more beef."

"For real?" Sage asks.

"We made up. And I'm over it. So, join the club."

Sage crosses her arms and frowns. "Uh, no thanks."

"Stop," I say to Sage. "I didn't do anything to you. And we're on the same team, so you're going to have to deal with me and not be rude."

"Way to make things awkward," Sage says.

"Not really," Tamar says. "I'm with Sarah. If Emilia is over what happened, then I am too. It's old news anyway."

"Whatever." Sage rolls her eyes.

I know I can't change what she or anyone else thinks of me. But it feels good to stand up for myself, and to know I'm right and say it out loud.

"Sarah!" Benny shouts from the other end of the hall. Ryan is standing next to him. "They're about to announce who made it onto the show."

I run over to them, and we walk into the crowded cafeteria together.

Sage, Tamar, and Emilia don't follow behind us. I guess

because they already know they didn't get picked and they don't care who did.

Chef Emily Ying is talking into the microphone about how everyone who competed today was amazing, and we should be proud of ourselves for giving the competition our all.

When she starts reading the names of the sixteen kids who've been selected for Chef Junior, Ryan grabs my hand. I don't think about what I'm doing; I reach over and grab Benny's hand too, and he holds mine back. There are butterflies in my stomach, fluttering in circles.

"In no particular order—Ellie Jacobs and CC Rodriguez, Miles Bam and Harrison Fisher, Anika Salem and Ronin Nagai, and Sam Dell and Oscar Matthews." That's four groups. *Breathe.* We're going to make it. We're good. There are still four spots left. That's a lot. "Isabella Hoffman and Lina Mercado." Three. "Sangeeta Chana and Elliot Strauss." Two. Benny squeezes my hand harder, like he wants me to know it will be okay. "Rosie Bell and Lily Turner. Sarah Weber and Benny Saraf—"

I don't hear what she says next, because Ryan is shrieking in my ear and jumping up and down. "YES! OMG! YES!" She hugs me and Benny, pulling us both in.

Benny's face lights up. "We did it!" He says it like he can't believe it's real.

But it is. It's real!

I reach out and hug him. He hugs me back and holds on, and I do too.

There's a rush of happiness and excitement and something else I can't remember ever feeling before now—confidence—pulsing through me. And I can't stop smiling, because I can feel how much I matter. Not just in this moment, but in everything. It doesn't feel like I got lucky or like it's going to disappear. It feels like I can be okay and take care of myself. I don't need to be afraid of not mattering, because I do. And I know I deserve to feel important and be loved and take up space, not just today, on a day I won, but every day.

AUTHOR'S NOTE

To my readers—

As I was writing *Taking Up Space*, there were many moments when I thought about walking away, because telling this story was painful. I was scared to be honest about the mixed-up way I saw myself growing up—as a person who wasn't worth being loved or being fed. Like Sarah, I felt I was taking up too much space in the world. And food was starting to take up all the space in my mind.

As a kid, I spent a lot of time comparing my problems to other people's struggles and convincing myself that what I was going through wasn't serious enough to matter, when in reality *everyone* deserves to get the help they need. Eventually, I did find the courage to ask for professional support, and I'm proud of how far I've come. I want you to know that I am still on this journey but I'm finally able to tell my story and advocate for others.

Taking Up Space is about what happens when the adults you rely on aren't always dependable. And how bad information about food and bodies can get twisted up in your mind and start to mess up the way you see everything—even yourself. This is happening to a lot of people—almost half of American and Canadian kids want to be thinner. It's about how puberty can make you feel uncomfortable but also strong. Ultimately, this book is about learning to trust that you're worth believing in and about finding the courage to stand up for what you deserve.

There isn't just one type of person impacted by low self-esteem, negative body image, disordered eating, and eating disorders. These challenges impact people of every age, size, weight, gender, race, sexual orientation, and socioeconomic status. You also can't look at someone and necessarily know if they're healthy or not. This means that many, many people face high barriers to getting the help they deserve. Listed here are resources where you can learn more:

National Eating Disorders Association (NEDA)
nationaleatingdisorders.org

Child Mind Institute
childmind.org/topics/concerns/eating-and-body-image/

Perhaps, like me, you have gotten used to diminishing your own pain, whatever your struggle might be, thinking that it is less significant than someone else's. There will always be someone whose challenges seem more urgent, but yours are still important too. If something negative is taking up space in your mind, even if there isn't a name for it, you can and should ask for help. I hope you will. You matter.

Love,
Alyson

ACKNOWLEDGMENTS

It took everything I had to write this book. I would never have had the courage to keep going if it were not for my amazing editors, Maya Marlette and David Levithan. Maya, thank you for encouraging me, pushing me, and cheering for me at each stage of this process. David, I'm not sure how I got so lucky to have you in my corner, but I'm very, very grateful.

This book would not exist without the constant support of Caela Carter, Amy Ewing, Jess Verdi, and Corey Haydu. Thank you to Jen Petro-Roy, who read an early draft, and to Tae Keller, who pointed me in the right direction and helped this story become the one I wanted to tell.

Since I started writing *Taking Up Space*, I have spent a lot of time with teachers and librarians. Thank you for everything you do for your students. Your work matters so much.

To the incredible team at Scholastic, thank you for supporting my books and getting them into the hands of kids: Ellie Berger, Lizette Serrano, Rachel Feld, Julia Eisler, Zakiya Jamal, Robin Hoffman, John Pels, Lori Benton, Jalen Garcia-Hall, Melissa Schirmer, Bill Franke, and Jackie Hornberger. Elizabeth Parisi and Baily Crawford, I appreciate all the extra work you did to make sure this cover represented the complicated story inside. And thank you to everyone in Clubs and Fairs, including Jana Haussmann, Kristin Standley, and Anna Swenson.

Thank you to my agent, Kate McKean, for believing in me.

Taking Up Space required a lot of experts: Special thanks to Danielle Lindner for your very thoughtful feedback and to Eric Goldberg, Sofia Ajodan, Chef Tali Friedman, Riley, Max, and Charlotte Dowell for advising. I'm grateful to my brother-in-law, Dann Kabala, and my sister-in-law, Tess Thompson, for answering my questions about basketball and college sports. And to my talented friend Rachelle Borer for always being willing to read and edit my work.

I'm lucky to have the best friends and family ever. Thank you for everything you do to support me. For this book, I called on Elise Dowell, Jaimie Mayer, Laine Blumenkopf, Stephanie Tankel, Nicola Bam, Leah Stoltz, Martha Hunt, and Brendan Cannon to help. Special thanks to Andrew's friends and family who have showed up and preordered books from New York, Minnesota, Pennsylvania, Arizona, the UK, and beyond. You know who you are, and I love you all.

Mom, you filled my world with books and modeled how to be brave. Your strength and love is in everything I do. Dad, thank you for being so proud of me always and for believing that I can accomplish whatever I want.

Thank you to my husband, Andrew, for being on this journey with me and for always having the long view. I love you.

Juliette, one day I'll tell you everything there is to know about me—about the moments I didn't think I'd make it and about the ones when I didn't think I mattered and about how I finally figured out how wrong I was about myself. Please know that struggling makes you strong, and it takes courage to believe in yourself and to take up space in the world. I love you.

ABOUT THE AUTHOR

Alyson Gerber is the author of the critically acclaimed, own-voices novels *Braced* and *Focused*. She is a graduate of The New School's MFA in Writing for Children and lives in Brooklyn, New York, with her husband and daughter. Visit her at alysongerber.com and find her everywhere else at @alysongerber.